George Vertue, Thomas Simon

Medals, coins, great seals, and other works of Thomas Simon

George Vertue, Thomas Simon

Medals, coins, great seals, and other works of Thomas Simon

ISBN/EAN: 9783742824837

Manufactured in Europe, USA, Canada, Australia, Japa

Cover: Foto ©Andreas Hilbeck / pixelio.de

Manufactured and distributed by brebook publishing software
(www.brebook.com)

George Vertue, Thomas Simon

Medals, coins, great seals, and other works of Thomas Simon

MEDALS, COINS, GREAT SEALS,

AND OTHER WORKS

OF

THOMAS SIMON:

ENGRAVED AND DESCRIBED

BY GEORGE VERTUE.

THE SECOND EDITION,

WITH ADDITIONAL PLATES AND NOTES,
AND AN APPENDIX BY THE EDITOR.

LONDON,

PRINTED BY J. NICHOLS, PRINTER TO THE SOCIETY OF ANTIQUARIES;

SOLD BY T. PAYNE AND SON; C. DILLY; H. PAYNE;
J. WALTER; AND N. CONANT.

MDCCLXXX.

PAX QVERITVR.

MEDALS,
COINS,
GREAT-SEALS
Impressions
from the Elaborate Works
of THOMAS SIMON, chief
Engraver of the MINT
to K. CHARLES the Ist
to the COMMONWEALTH
the Lord PROTECTOR
CROMWELL,
and in the Reign
of K. CHARLES II
to
MDCLXV
by Geo.

Invented and Published by Geo. Vertue according to Act of Parliament Nov.17.17

To the Honourable

JAMES WEST, Esq.

Secretary to his Majesty's

TREASURY,

One of the VICE PRESIDENTS

of the ROYAL SOCIETY,

and of the SOCIETY of ANTIQUARIES

LONDON.

HONOURABLE SIR,

THE following COLLECTIONS of the WORKS of that great Artiſt THOMAS SIMON, ſo much admired for their Exellency and Rarity, it has been my Happineſs to view with great Pleaſure, in the choice Cabinets of ſeveral curious Noblemen and Gentlemen; eſpecially thoſe in your Poſſeſſion.

UPON

UPON my firſt Intention of publiſhing them together, from a Motion by yourſelf made to me, that ſuch a Work would be acceptable to the Publick; and conſidering it with my frequent Inſpections of thoſe rare Performances by Mr. SIMON and his BROTHER, I reſolved to bring the ſame, in the following Manner, to a Concluſion.

YOUR friendly Aſſiſtance to forward this Deſign, has been of the greateſt uſe to me; and will both give ſome Idea of their Operations ſo much valued and eſteemed, and alſo commemorate many notable Facts of thoſe mutable Times. Therefore, with your Encouragement, this Communication to the Publick is humbly inſcribed by,

HONOURABLE SIR,

Your ever obliged

and reſpectful Servant,

George Vertue.

The Engraved PLATES
contained in this WORK.

A 2   VI.

[5]

O B S E R-

OBSERVATIONS

TO THE CURIOUS

R E A D E R.

THE collecting of Coins and Medals is known to be a noble Amusement; the Delight of the Curious, a good Ornament to History, as well as a necessary Appendage to Books of that kind. Many Nations in former Ages, as well as the present, have Experience in this Subject; and it is allowed and encouraged in all polite Nations. From whence is seen and known the great Honour, Pleasure, and Usefulness of such Studies; for which no Argument need be advanced, where the Fact is past Dispute.

For these and many more Reasons, it has been often desired and wished, that an account of our National Coins, Medals, &c. with their Delineations engraved, printed, and published, were justly done. First, for our own Satisfaction, in honour of our Country; which might appear to other parts of the learned World with as much Lustre, as the Grandeur and Power of this Kingdom doth appear on other occasions.

As

As it is evident, from many noble Collections, already made amongſt the Curious, with great Diligence and Expence, ſuch is the Variety and Scarcity of Coins as now renders it almoſt impracticable for one Perſon to collect an intire Series of all the different kinds that have been from the *Norman Conqueſt*, through ſo many Ages, to the preſent Time :.

Yet the whole may be compleated, or conceived, from the ſeveral Cabinets of Noblemen and others, as a moſt worthy Gentleman * has of late Years printed a very accurate account of our Engliſh Coins with the greateſt exactneſs, and has alſo proceeded in cauſing moſt of thoſe Coins to be engraven, with juſt care and minute obſervations.

Of theſe affairs I have long conſidered ſince I have had the Honour of being a Member of a Society of Gentlemen, whoſe kind aſſiſtance enabled me to undertake this part of ſuch a curious Work, eſpecially as I have for many years had free acceſs to ſeveral rare Collections, and Cabinets of Medals and Coins, and my own Obſervations of theſe Works, with Broad Seals of the Common-wealth of *England*; containing chiefly thoſe done by *T. Simon*, the famous Engraver of the Mint in *London*,

* *Martin Folkes*, Eſq.

Exegi

Exegi Monumentum Ære perennius. Hor.

This curious Part, in hopes to compleat, is according to my beft Endeavours, wherein is contained many remarkable Works, relating to thofe Times, of publick Actions and Per-fons noted for their Service of the State and Government of *England*, during the Civil Wars, till the Reftoration of the Royal Family.

Wherein will be exhibited Samples of our firft milled Mo-nies, Coins and Medals of the utmoft Delicacy, of excellent Workmanfhip, which are allowed to be an Honour to this Nation.

This Opportunity I have taken, as moft convenient alfo, to reprefent the true Draughts and Delineations of feveral Broad Seals of the Common-wealth of *England*, *Ireland*, and *Scotland*, which were never yet publifhed; and are equally the Admiration of the Curious; being highly prized, when the Impreffions of them are fair and well preferved; as many and moft of them are; for perfecting whereof I have had all poffible Opportunities, in Enquiries and Affiftance neceffary, by many Years Study and Obfervation to adorn this Work.

It is here only propofed to publifh the Prints of thefe, from fuch Collections, without any Obfervations, concerning right or wrong, juft or unjuft, leaving that to the impartial

B   Readers

Readers of the beſt authentick Writers; only having drawn out in ſome Sort of Succeſſion the Works done to commemorate Acts of thoſe Times, wherein *T. Simon*, or his Brother *Abraham Simon*, were concerned, to illuſtrate I hope thereby ſome Parts in Hiſtory, and to hand to Poſterity the Fame of thoſe excellent and much admired Artiſts.

THE

THE extraordinary Events of the Government of this Kingdom of *England*, and that of *Scotland*, and *Ireland*, are fully related in the Annals and Hiftories of thofe Times, concerning King *Charles* the Firft, in the latter Part of his Reign, with the Civil Wars and Eftablifhment of the *Common-wealth*, and many Volumes, Books, and Pamphlets have been written, and publifhed; but without fuch additional Delineations as printed Sculptures, to illuftrate feveral material Points by Draughts taken exactly from the Medals, Coins, and Broad Seals.

The Want of thefe neceffary Tables or Infignia has been my long Study to fupply, by fearching after, and collecting the various Impreffions in Gold and Silver, or thofe in Wax, affixed to Deeds, or Proofs in any other Materials, of the Works of *Thomas Simon* chief Engraver of the Mint, firft in King *Charles* the Firft's Time, and afterwards, when he was more particularly by the Parliament employed in the fame Office, to be chief Engraver alfo of the Mint, and Seals, &c. for the Ufe of the *Common-wealth*.

As to his Employment in the Reign of King *Charles* the Firft. I fhall treat more diftinctly thereof, in the Part referved for fome perfonal Particulars of his Life; and only obferve here, that he was initiated into Bufinefs after Monfieur *Briot*, who was Engraver for the Mint, returned into *France*; being recommended into his Place by Sir *Edward Harley*, Mafter of the Mint, under whom he graved fome Dyes for Coins, Medals, and Seals for the Government. Particularly about the year

B 2   1636,

1636, he finifhed a moſt curious Great Seal for the Admiralty, when *Algernon Sidney*, Earl of *Northumberland*, was Lord High Admiral. This, and others of his accurate Performances, recommended him afterwards to the Commonwealth, when they propoſed to have a Great Seal, and others, for their Uſe, and the Parliament.

After the Siege and Surrender of the City of *Oxford*, in 1646, to Sir *Thomas Fairfax* the Parliament General, when the King's State Seals were taken there, and ordered to be ſent up to the Parliament, they were broken in the Preſence of the Lords and Commons there aſſembled, on the Eleventh of *Auguſt* that Year. Their Proceedings to conſtitute a new Seal, under their own Authority, may appear in the following Extract thereof, from their own Journals.

" *Die Sabbati*, 6 *Januarii*, 1648 ª.

Mr. *Love*, Mr. *Blakiſton*, Mr. *Scot*, Mr. *Purefoy*, Mr. *Millington*, Lord *Munſon*, Mr. *Fry*, Mr. *Allen*, Colonel *Marten*;

This Committee, or any two of them, are to take Order for the framing of a Great Seal ; and are to bring in the Form thereof, on *Monday* Morning next :

The more particular Care hereof is referred to Mr. *Henry Marten*.

Die Veneris, 26 *Januarii*, 1648.

Ordered,

That *Thomas Simon* be hereby authorized to engrave a Seal, according to the Form formerly directed.

From the printed *Journals of the Houſe of Commons*.

Ordered,

4

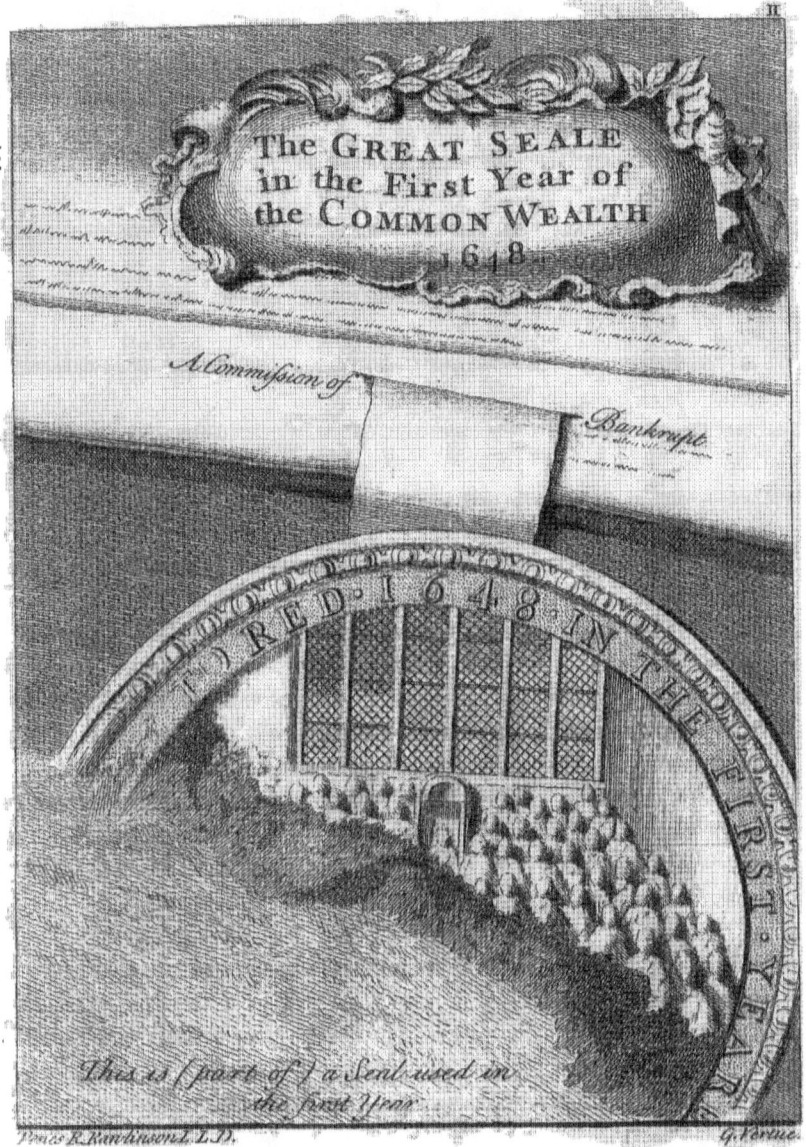

Ordered,

That *Thomas Simon* fhall have the Sum of two hundred Pounds, for graving the faid Great Seal, and for the Materials thereof.

Die Sabbati, 3 *Februarii,* 1648.

Ordered,

That the Seal of the Court of *Exchequer* be altered in like Manner, as the Great Seal is altered : and that the Title of the faid Seal be from henceforth, SIGILLUM. SCACCARII. PUBLICI : and that the Writs and Procefs to iffué out of the faid Court, which bear Date the laft Day of *Michaelmas* Term laft, and the three and twentieth Day of *January* laft, fhall be fealed with the Old *Exchequer* Seal.

And it is referred to the former Committee, appointed to prepare the Great Seal, to prepare an Act for that Purpofe : And they are alfo to prepare an Act for the Alteration of all other Seals belonging to the feveral Courts in *Weftminfter-hall* : and they are likewife to confider of the antedating of Writs."

The Alterations of thefe, and other Seals, for the Courts of Juftice, and publick Offices, being made according to thefe Orders, it was a long time before I could obtain an impreffion of the firft great Seal, which was graved according to their Appointment, and circumfcribed in the *firft Year* of the Common-wealth. It was impreffed on Wax, and fixed to a Deed; having, on one fide, this Infcription or Legend round it, IN. THE. FIRST. YEARE. OF. FREEDOME. BY. GOD's. BLESSING. RESTORED. 1648. *Vide* Plate II. reprefenting the Houfe of Commons fitting, with the Speaker in the Chair. The other fide, undoubtedly dated the fame Year, and reprefenting a Map of *England*, &c. being imperfectly impreffed,

preſſed, and defaced in the Wax, is not, in this Plate, engraved; but may be ſeen, from a more perfect Impreſſion,
Plate VI. On the 7th of *February* that Year, this Great Seal
was brought into the Houſe, and delivered to the Commiſſion-
ers then appointed, who were *Whitlock*, *Keeble*, and *Liſle* [b].

One of thoſe, mentioned in the Order aforeſaid, to be
formed for the Uſe of the *Common Bench*, is much alike on both
ſides to the Great Seal, *Vide* Plate III ; but the circumſcription on one ſide is, SIGILLUM. PRO. BREVIBUS CORAM. JUSTI-
CIARIIS. COMMUNIS. BANCI. 1648. And on the other ſide,
IN. THE. FIRST. YEARE. OF. FREEDOME. BY. GOD'S. BLESSING.
RESTORED. 1648 [c].

Plate IV. The Seal for the County Palatine of *Lancaſter*,
containing two ornamented Shields conjoined; one, bearing
the Croſs of *England*, and the other, the Harp for *Ireland*;
with this Circumſcription. THE. SEAL. OF. THE. COUNTY.
PALATINE. OF. LANCASTER. 1648. The other ſide, the
Houſe ſitting ; THE. FIRST. YEARE. OF. FREEDOME. BY. GOD'S.
BLESSING. RESTORED. 1648 [d].

Plate V. Another Seal, of the *Duchy* of *Lancaſter*, repreſenting two Eſcucheons conjoined ; the Croſs of *England* in
one, and the Harp of *Ireland*, in the other, encircled with a
Wreath of Laurel, and circumſcribed, THE. SEAL. OF. THE.
DUCHY. OF LANCASTER. 1648 [e].

In the ſame Plate are engraved two Seals for the uſe of
the Parliament. In one, are two Shields joined together, con-

[b] The Impreſſion of this Seal is ſix Inches diameter, and it is affixed to a Commiſſion
of Bankruptcy againſt *Daniel Gotherſon* and *Francis Soane*, *April*, 1651, in the Poſſeſſion
of *R. Rawlinſon*, L.L.D.
[c] This Seal is four Inches diameter, and was communicated to me by *James Weſt*, Eſq.
[d] From a Deed in the Poſſeſſion of *Eraſmus Earl*, Eſq.
[e] From an Impreſſion in my own Collection.

taining

The SEAL for the COURT
of COMMON BENCH
at Westminster
A. D^m MDCXLVIII

The SEAL for the COMMON PLEAS
for the County Palatine
of LANCASTER

Vertue.

The Parliament Seal

another Seal

The SEAL of the Dutchy of Lancaster, 1648,
and the Parliaments SEALS 1649 were most probably
done for the Uses proposed by Parliament.

The GREAT-SEAL *of the* Common-Wealth *of* ENGLAND.

done by Tho: Simon

THE IRISH

THE BRITISH SEAS

This Engrav'd from a Curious Proof-Impression in Wax which was in the Collection of the R.t Hon.ble y.e EARL of OXFORD; now in Possession of her Grace the DUTCHESS of PORTLAND.

most humbly inscrib'd by G. Virtue.

taining the *Englijh* Crofs, and the *Irijh* Harp; with this Cir-
cumfcription : THE. SEALE. OF. THE. PARLIAMENT. OF. THE.
COMMONWEALTH. OF. ENGLAND [f] : In the other, appears the
Houfe of Commons fitting, with the Speaker; circumfcribed
PARLIAMENTUM. ANGLIÆ. ANNO. DOMINI. 1649 [g].

On *March* 26, 1650, there was an Act paffed for making
a new Great Seal, for the Ufe of the Parliament, inftead of
the firft, made in the firft Year of the Common-wealth. The
fmall time our Artift had to defign and engrave the firft great
Seal made it appear a furprizing Performance: the Prepara-
tion only of a Report being ordered for forming that Great
Seal, on the 9th of *January* 1648; and it was delivered to
the Commiffioners on the 7th of *February* following.

It may be here proper to explain to the Reader fome difference obferved in that of the Firft, and this of the third
Year, Plate VI. which is circumfcribed, THE. GREAT. SEAL.
OF. ENGLAND. 1651; and is the moft curious and extraordinary work that was ever performed, as may be feen by the
fair Impreffions, whereof fome few were taken off by *Simon*
himfelf; one of which is here engraved, and had been in
the Collection of the late Right Honourable *Edward* Earl of
Oxford. On the fide of this new Great Seal, which has that
Circumfcription, there is a Map of *England* and *Ireland*, more
accurately reprefented, with the Iflands, Sea Ports, Counties,
Cities, Towns, &c. of thefe Kingdoms; fo diftinctly expreffed
and named in fuch minute Characters, as to make it a work
truly admirable, and beyond compare. Between the two
Iflands is engraved in Capitals, THE IRISH SEA; and, in the

[f] The Diameter of this Seal is two Inches and half, communicated by *Smart Lethieul-
lier*, Efq. who exhibited it to the Society of Antiquaries 1736-7.
[g] This Seal is three Inches over, and belongs to *R. Dingley*, Efq.

lower

lower Part, THE BRITISH SEA; which are not fo diftinguifhed in the firft Seal: The other fide, Plate VII. reprefents the Houfe of Commons fitting, with the Speaker in his Chair, as alfo in the former; but the great Window at the end of the Houfe is not quite fo large, as in the other: And the Circumfcription hereon, is

IN. THE. THIRD. YEARE. OF. FREEDOME. BY. GOD'S. BLES-
SING. RESTORED. 1651 [h].

Both thefe Plates were infcribed to her Grace, *Margaret* Duchefs of *Portland*, who obliged me with the Favour of communicating them in this manner to the public.

Soon after the King's Death, the Common-wealth, finding it neceffary to eftablifh their Power and Reputation, thought it convenient to have Monies coined with their Stile and Authority, appointing the fame to be made of the Gold and Silver Plate, which had been feized in the King's Houfhold, or Treafury. All which was carried to the Mint, in the Tower of London, according to Directions from the Parliament and Council of State, to the Amount of many thoufand Pounds [i]. Their Order is dated the 13th of *February* 1648-9. *Vide* Plate VIII.

The filver hammered Money of the Commonwealth.

Thereon was ftamp'd the Arms or *Infignia* for *England*, on a Shield, encircled with a Palm and a Laurel Branch: infcribed,

[h] This Great Seal, as ufual, is fix Inches over.
[i] As appears by the ftated Accounts of the King's Inventory of Plate, Jewels, Goods, Pictures, &c. taken by Order of Parliament, *Anno* 1649. Of all which Particular, I have procured Copies and Tranfcripts, from the feveral Lifts and Inventories thereof, with Intention to publifh the fame, when Opportunity permits.

THE

VII
The GREAT-SEAL of the
Common-Wealth of ENGLAND.
done by Tho: Simon.
IN THE THIRD YEARE OF FREEDOME BY GODS BLESSING RESTORED 1651
EARL of OXFORD
MARGARET CAVENDISHE DUTCHESS of PORTLAND
1744.

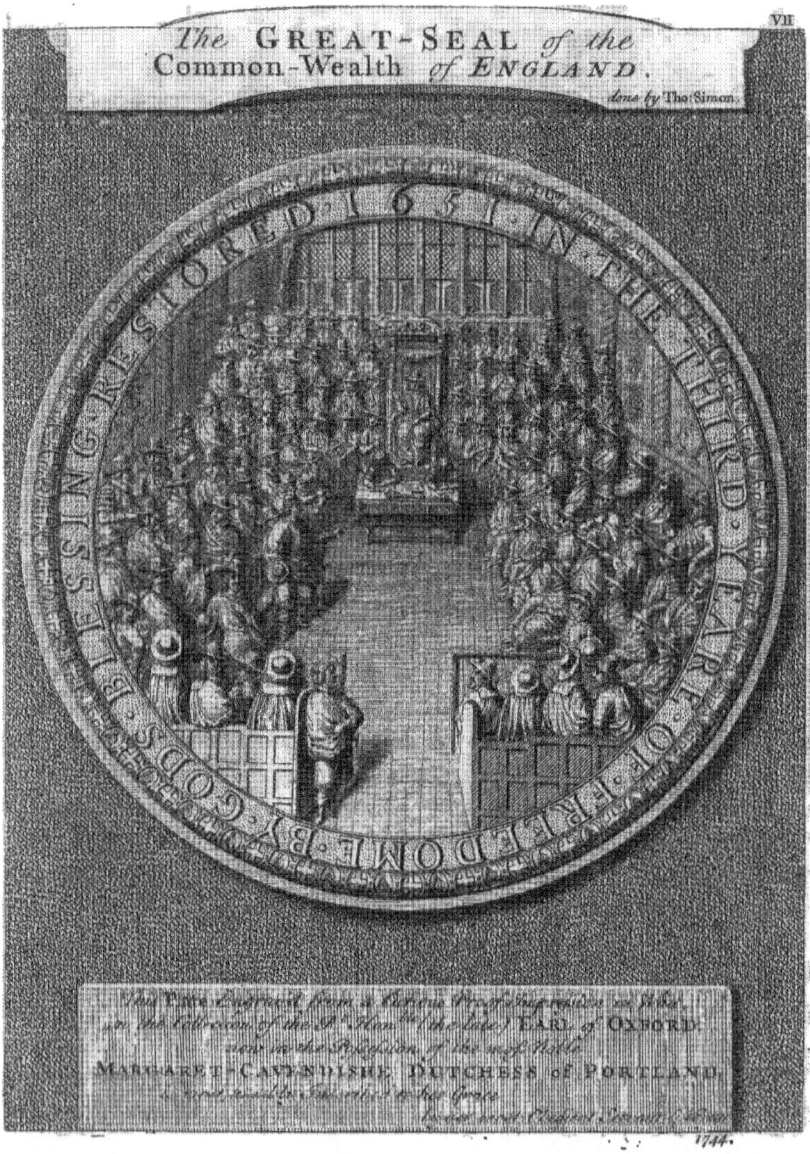

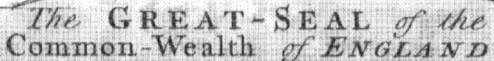

Common-Wealth Coins of Silver.

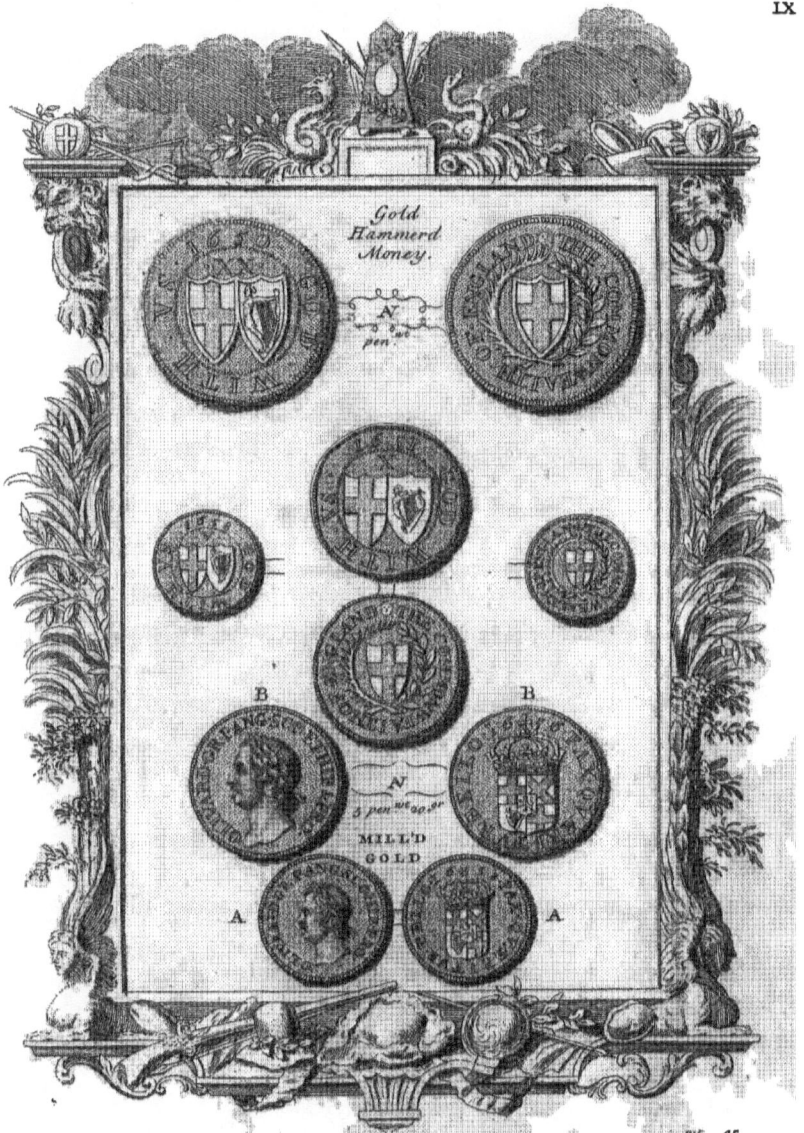

Gold
Hammerd
Money.

MILL'D
GOLD

B   B

A   A

A.A. *Some rare Gold Pieces mill'd & from the same Dye.* 10. pen.ᵗᵉ 4.ᵍʳ

THE. COMMONWEALTH. OF. ENGLAND.

with a figure of the Sun for the Mint Mark: the other fide has two Shields joined; in one, is a Crofs for *England*, and in the other, a Harp for *Ireland*; circumfcribed

GOD. WITH. US. 1649.

Over the two Shields, is, the numerical letter V. which fignifies the five Shilling Piece, being of the fame Weight and Standard with the former Crown Pieces.

On the II and VI penny Pieces we have the like Device.

Alfo in the XII and the VI penny Pieces; being likewife of the fame Weight and Standard, as the former coined Monies were.

Gold Coins of the Common-wealth's Money.

PLATE IX. The XX Shilling Piece of Gold; two Shields, with the Badges of *England* and *Ireland*; circumfcribed

GOD. WITH. US. 1650.

On the other Side, a Crofs in a Shield encircled with a Palm and Laurel Branch; circumfcribed

THE. COMMON-WEALTH. OF. ENGLAND.

The X Shilling and V Shilling Pieces in Gold bear the fame Figure and Infcriptions.

In the fame Plate are Gold Coins, very beautifully milled in the fkrew Prefs; one with a grained Edge; (A) reprefenting, on one Side, the Head of *Oliver Cromwell*, in profile, laureated, and circumfcribed thus

C   OLIVAR.

OLIVAR. D. G. R. P. ANG. SCO. ET. HIB, &c. PRO.

The Reverfe, a Scutcheon, quarterly; firft, the Crofs of *England*; fecond, the Crofs of *Scotland*; third, the Harp of *Ireland*; and the fourth as the firft. In the middle a fcutcheon of pretence containing a Lion rampant, the paternal arms of the *Cromwells*: Over all, the Crown of *England*, circumfcribed

PAX. QUÆRITUR. BELLO. 1658 [h].

Some of thefe are dated 1656; a few others, a little larger and heavier [i]; with the fame head of *Oliver*, (B) Infcription and Reverfe; (B) alfo of the fame date. And on the Edge, fairly ftruck, this Motto,

PROTECTOR. LITERIS. LITERÆ. NUMMIS. CORONA. ET. SALUS [*]

Thefe Gold milled pieces are, all of them, rare; but one moft extraordinary, which I have heard of, is of the weight of fix Broad Pieces.

[h] 5 Penny-weights, 21 Grains.
[i] 14 Penny-weights, 15 Grains.
[*] Mr. *Weft* fhewed one of them at the Antiquary Society, 1734.

Meda

MEDALS of SILVER

Medals of the EARL *of* ESSEX, *in Silver.*

PLATE X. An oval Medal, (A) reprefenting the Houfe of Lords, with the King in Parliament; and the Houfe of Commons with their Speaker. On the other fide, is the Earl of *Effex* in armour, with his fword in his right hand; circumfcribed, in the inward circle,

Pro Religione, Rege, Lege, et Parliamento.

And in the outward circle,

For the Religion and the Subjects Freedom, behold here both Houfes of Parliament.

Another oval Medal (B) of the fame General, reprefenting, on one fide, the Houfes of Lords and Commons as in the fore-mentioned Medal; the Circumfcription, upon a border*,

IN. THE. MULTITUDE. OF. COUNCELLORS. THERE. IS. PEACE.

On the other fide, the General with his fword, and a right hand holding another fword over his head; circumfcribed

THE. SWORD. OF. THE. LORD. AND. OF. GYDEON.

Another fmaller oval Medal (C) only his Head, a full face; the Reverfe, containing the arms of *D'Evreux*, with a Coronet on the top.

Another Medal, in a circle, (D); reprefenting the General in armour; circumfcribed,

∴ R. R. R. P. P. P. FIDISSIMUS, 1644.

---

* Mr. *Ames* fhewed fuch an one at the Antiquary Society, 1741; the head in a wreath or civic crown, and over it S. X. Mr. *Nixon*, of *Lombard-ftreet*, had another fuch fhewn there by *P. Wright*, 1773.

On

On the Reverſe **S. X.** in large capitals, with a Scroll beneath inſcribed, **G. L.** for *Generalis Legionis.* And circum-ſcribed

MAG. PROTEC[R]. LIBERTAT[V]. PATRIÆ.

The Earl reſigned his Commiſſion to the Parliament in *April,* 1645.

The laſt of theſe is a ſmall curious oval Medal in Gold, ſtruck upon the death of the Earl; repreſenting, on one ſide, his Buſt in profile, inſcribed

ROB. ESSEX. COM. MIL. PARL. DUX. GEN.

And below the Buſt, **T. S. F.** for *Thomas Simon fecit.* On the Reverſe, round a Figure of Grief, with a broken Column, inſcribed, **F. E. R. T.**[k], there is this legend,

HINC. ILLE. LACHRYMÆ.

In the Exergue.

ABRUP. SEP. 14. 1646.

In his Place, Sir *Thomas Fairfax* was declared General; and *Oliver Cromwell,* Lieutenant General.

---

[k] To ſignify, *Fortitudo Ejus Rhodum Tenuit.*

Medals

MEDALS of GOLD and SILVER.

Medals of General FAIRFAX, *in Silver and in Gold.*

PLATE XI.   A Medal, ftruck in honour of *Ferdinand* Lord *Fairfax*, Father of Sir *Thomas Fairfax*, in an Oval of Silver, with an embofſed border of foliage about it (F) containing his Buft in armour; the Reverfe, his arms, a Lion rampant over three Bars Sable.

Another fmaller Silver Medal in Oval, (G) with his Head, and a laced fcolloped Band; the Reverfe, his Arms as before, circumfcribed

FERD. LORD. FAIRFAX. LORD. GFNERAL. OF. THE NORTH.

Another, much like it, of his fon, (H) his Head, with a plain fhort Band, and the fame Arms, on the Reverfe; circumfcribed;

SIR. THOMAS. FAIRFAX. KNT. FOR. KING. AND. PARL.

The next, in Oval, (I) is the moft curious Medal in Gold; with the Head in profile, of General *Fairfax*; the Infcription about it,

THO. FAIRFAX. MILES. MILIT. PARL. DUX. GEN.

The Reverfe, infcribed in the middle,

MERUISTI.

And round about it;

POST. HAC. MELIORA. 1645.

The fame Head in a fmaller Oval of gold, (K) without any Circumfcription; but, on the Reverfe, the fame Legend as before.   Thefe two laft are frequently feen in the Cabinets
of

of the Curious, and were also in the Possession of the late *Bryan Fairfax* Esquire *.

LL. The very same profile of *Fairfax*, faintly struck in a circular Medal of Silver; circumscribed

GENERAL. FAIRFAX.

On the other side, the Head of *Oliver* in profile, very boldly struck out, and circumscribed

OLIVAR. D. GR. ANG. SCO. HIB. & PROT.

These two Heads on one Medal seem to have been thus artfully struck, to indicate the Decline of General *Fairfax*, and the Uprising of *Oliver* to the *Protectorate*. And it may be further observed, that this Head of *Oliver* is

---

* Mr. *Bartlet* shewed the Society of Antiquaries copies of Certificates given by Sir *Thomas Fairfax* to *John Sharpe* of *Horton*, in the Parish of *Bradford, Torkshire*, an Officer of his Army. The Originals are on Parchment; one dated 1645, the other 1647.

The Seal and Arms of *Fairfax* on Wafer.	" I do acknowledge that *John Sharpe* hath deservedly received a Medall from the Parliament and Citty of *London*, in remembrance of his faithful Service under my Command, in the Year 1645. *Fairfax*."
The Seal and Arms of *Fairfax* in Wax.	" Sir *Thomas Fairfax* Knight, Commander in Chiefe of all the Land-Forces under the Pay of the Parliament, within the Kingdom of *England*, Dominion of *Wales*, and in the Islands of *Guernsey* and *Jersey*, in order to the Peace and Security of the Kingdom, reducing of *Ireland*, and disbanding of such as shall be thought fitt by both Houses.

I·do hereby acknowledge that Mr. *John Sharpe* hath deservedly received a Medall from the Parliament and Citty of *London*, in remembrance of his faithful Service under my Command.

Given under my Hand and Seal att *Kingston*, the 30 Day of *August* 1647.

FAIRFAX."

Mr. *Bartlet* says, that of these two Medals, the Silver one is the larger, and is the same with that given in *Evelyn*, p. 116. The Gold one wants the Inscription round the Head, but the reverses of both are the same. MERUISTI. POST. HÆC. MELIORA. 1645. From these certificates it appears by whose appointment and at whose expence these Medals were struck, about which the Historians and Medallists of the time give so little Information. Vertue, Plate XI. gives four Medals of *Fairfax*, the largest like that in *Evelyn*, a Gold, as is the smallest of the two here mentioned.

struck

Several MEDALS *of* OLIVER CROMWEL.

ſtruck with the ſame Puncheon as that of his figure on Horſeback in his Great Seal. *Vide* Plate XVII *.

Medals of OLIVER CROMWELL.

P L A T E XII. An oval Medal in Silver of General *Crom-well*, (A) a Profile; under the Shoulder, *Tho. Simon*, F. The Motto about the Head,

WORD. AT.} THE. LORD. OF. HOSTS. {SEPTEM-
DUNBAR.   {Y^r. 3. 1650.

Behind the Head, a Proſpect of the Battle. The Reverſe, is the Houſe of Commons ſitting; as repreſented on the Parliament Great Seal 1648, and alſo on that Great Seal of the Commonwealth of *England*, 1651. This Medal, it is thought, was ſtruck by *Oliver's* own appointment; being the firſt drawn for him from the Life by *Simon*; and is remarkable for his Likeneſs when Lieutenant General [I]; as appears by comparing it with a Picture of him drawn by *Walker*, his Painter, about that time. The profile of this Medal differs in ſome reſpects from that Medal (B) copied by *Simon* alſo from a curious Limning drawn by *Samuel Cooper*; the Original

---

* This Medal was ſhewn by Mr. *Virtue* at the Antiquary Society 1745, from the Collection of Commiſſioner *Fairfax*. Under *Fairfax's* Head a ſmall T. S. F. (*Thomas Simon fecit*.)

[I] The Dye of this Medal was kept in the Family; for there was an Houſe in the County of *Hants*, where his Son *Richard* once lived; which being purchaſed by one of the *Heathcotes*, there was lately found, in pulling it down, the ſaid Dye in the Walls thereof.

*** This Eſtate at *Hurſley*, eight Miles from *Wincheſter*, the only one which the Government could not ſeize, being ſettled in Jointure on *Richard Cromwell's* Wife, was ſold to the late Sir *William Heathcote*, who, it was pretended, made a vow that not a ſtone or brick of *Oliver Cromwell's* Houſe ſhould ſtand even in the foundations, and accordingly pulled it entirely down, and in part of the Wall the dye of a Seal was found by a workman, who brought it to him at *Wincheſter*, where he then lived. He ſold it for a Roman Weight; it being very ruſty. It was ſoon cleaned, and diſcovered by the Inſcription to be the Seal of the Parliament of the Common-wealth of *England*; by which Mr. *Virtue*, who ſaw it 1741, among the Medals of a Mrs. *Roberts*, ſuppoſed it to be the very Seal which *Oliver* took from the Parliament. (Ant. Soc. Min. vol. IV. p. 78.)

I

whereof is preferved in the Collection of the Duke of *Devon-fhire*. The minute Reprefentation of the Houfe of Commons in this Medal is very extraordinary; but much more fo in another Medal much lefs, which contains alfo the General's Head and Infcription, and on the Reverfe, the Parliament fitting. Both thefe are frequently feen in Silver, and fometimes in Gold; and when fairly ftruck, and well preferved, do great honour to the ingenious Artift who engraved thefe curious and memorable Medals.

Another oval Medal, (C) with his Head in front, boldly projected. About it is infcribed

OLI. CROMWELL. MILIT. PARL. DUX. GEN.

A few being ftruck, there appeared a flaw or crack in the fteel dye, for which reafon it was not much ufed; or, as it was performed about the time that he was Lieutenant General, and before he advanced to be Lord Protector, the Stile being already cut, could not be altered, and therefore it was difufed and laid by, without any Reverfe made to it. This Dye, it is faid, was conveyed into *Holland* about thirty Years fince, and many were ftruck off in Silver, &c. And, though cracked, the Medal fold for an high Price here. So great was the profit made of it, that another was imitated after it, (C) but in a Circle, and probably at *Geneva*, wherein the Head was copied fo exactly, and the letters T.S. on it, that it paffes for the Original, though it differs alfo in the Infcription, which is

OLIV. D. G. R. P. ANG. SCO. ET. HIB. PRO.

When this was done, to make a Reverfe to it, they have copied from another Medal, reprefenting a Lion feiant, holding a Scutcheon of Arms. *Vide* (R)

A fmall

A fmall oval Medal (D) with the Head of *Oliver*, circum-fcribed

HITHERTO. HATH. THE. LORD. HELPED. US.

This I do not imagine to be the Work of *Simon*.

But the fair, round, and large Medal (E. E) of the Protector in profile, is certainly genuine; fometimes feen in Silver, and one I have feen in Gold ᵐ, reprefenting an elegant bufto of him in profile, thus circumfcribed,

OLIVARUS. DEI. GRA. REIPUB. ANGLIÆ. SCO. ET. HIB.
PROTECTOR. THO. SIMON. F.

On the Reverfe, a Lion *Seiant*, with the Arms, quarterly, of *England, Scotland,* and *Ireland :* with a Scutcheon of Pretence in the middle, containing the Arms of *Cromwell*; and the In-fcription,

PAX. QUÆRITUR. BELLO.

(F) A curious fmall Gold Medal in oval; ftruck in memory of the *Obiit* of *Oliver Cromwell*; reprefenting his Buft laure-ated and in armour, circumfcribed,

OLIVAR. D. G. R. P. ANG. SCO. HIB. ET. PROTECTO.——

The Reverfe, an *Olive* tree, with this infcription round it,

NON. DEFITIENT. OLIVA. SEP. 3. 1658.

Thefe Medals were, in all likelihood, ftruck to be given away at his pompous Funeral to his friends and followers ⁿ.

Another Medal of *Oliver* (G) and the Reverfe like the for-mer, but larger, and in a circle ; and there is about the neck a little drapery, inftead of armour. This medal of *Cromwell*, being ftruck feveral years after his death, to gra-

---

ᵐ In the Collection of the late Mr. *Thomas Granger*.

ⁿ One of thefe Medals was in the Collection of the late Earl of *Oxford*, and another in that of the late Sir *Hans Sloane*.

D

tify

tify his admirers, appears in the head, face, and drapery, to be an imitation probably done in *Holland*, of his milled Shilling; 'tis circumfcribed, as the laft medal, (F) with the fame motto and date; which was the day and year of *Oliver's* death. A day remarkable to him; being that on which he fought the battle at *Dunbar*, 1650. and on which he obtained the victory at *Worcefter*, 1651.

Befides thefe, there is a Gold Medalion, the largeft of all with the fame Head and Reverfe, but of groffer workmanfhip; therefore not here reprefented among *Simon's* Performances °. It fold at an auction for ten Guineas, being no more than its weight.

As I do not propofe to mention any Medals of the Lord Protector but what are done by *Simon*, therefore, though I have feen one amongft the feries of medals of the Kings of *England*, on account of its having been done among thofe *Geneva* I have not defcribed it in this work.

° But in *Evelyn*, p. 119.

The

The Common-wealth's milled Monies.

THE Council of State and Commons in Parliament having had it reprefented to them, that the coins of this Government might be more perfectly and beautifully done, and made equal to any coins in *Europe*, propofed to fend to *France* for an artift, who had invented and improved a machine, and method to make all coins, by a *fcrew Prefs* and *Mill*, with the moft beautiful polifh, and equality on the edge, or any proper infcription, or graining, which might denote the time of coining, or prevent the falfifying of coins, or their being clipt (as ufually) and counterfeited P.

" By the Council of State, ordered 8th of *Auguft* 1649 to fend for *Peter Blondeau*, from *Paris*, to come to *London*, to treat with him, upon the price and expence of coining money after his new Invention." He arrived at *London Sept.* 3, 1649, being allowed for his journey and expences.

" By the Council of State, a Committee of the Mint was appointed to examine all the circumftances of the way of coining propounded by *Blondeau*. And having heard all objections that could be alledged by the Mafters, Officers, and Workmen of the Mint, the faid Committee concluded, and voted, that the manner of coining by *Blondeau* was better, more advantageous, and honourable for the State, than that which was already ufed by the Common-wealth." But the Moniers of the Mint made fuch a ftrong oppofition to this

P See *T. Violet's* Myfteries and Secrets of Trade and the Mint.

Re-

Refolution, notwithſtanding what the Committee had appointed, that *Blondeau* could not proceed for fome time.

However, feveral fpecimens were made and produced,
finely wrought, and milled; having a moſt beautiful poliſh,
and grained round the edges; fome of them impreſſed on the
edge.

Plate XIII. (A) Of thefe pieces thus coined, one was the
Half Crown, containing on one fide, the Crofs in a Shield,
with a Palm and Laurel about it, circumſcribed,

THE COMMON-WEALTH. OF. ENGLAND.

And on the other fide, the Crofs and Harp, within two
Efcutcheons; and over them, II. VI. infcribed about,

GOD. WITH. US. 1651.

With this Infcription round the edge,

TRUTH. AND. PEACE. 1651. PETRUS. BLONDEUS. INVENTOR.
FECIT.

In other refpects, the fame as the hammered money made
current by the Government of the Common-wealth.

The Shilling, or XII pence, (B) coined in the fame manner,
with the fame Arms, Motto, Infcription, Date, and grained Edge.

Alfo a fmall Piece of VI Pence, (C) of the fame kind and
form; all neatly and perfectly performed; the Half Crown
has the impreſſed Infcription and Name of the Inventor on
the edge.

The Council of State having confidered *Blondeau's* trouble,
beſtowed on him Forty Pounds *Sterling*. And Mr. *Froſt*, then
Secretary to the Council, told *Blondeau*, before feveral Wit-
neſſes, that, if the State could not agree with him about the
price, and that he fhould be neceſſitated to withdraw himfelf,

Common-Wealth Milld Monies.

felf, the State would - indemnify him for his journey, both coming and returning.

Still the *Moniers* of the Mint, being a Corporation in the *Tower of London*, contefted againft *Blondeau*, that they would produce monies wrought of equal perfection, and beauty; by which they got further time to perform it, and dive into his Invention. After feveral debates and reprefentations, they objected, that thofe pieces fent by *Blondeau* to the Council of State, were not, probably, performed wholly by himfelf; befides, that it was an old Invention, which they themfelves knew how to do ; and that fuch pieces were only made for curiofity ⁹. It is thought that *Simon* fecretly graved the dyes for *Blondeau*, though he invented the machine, the infcription on the edge, and the beautiful polifh.

Thereupon was prefented the following propofition of the *Provoft*, and *Moniers* of the *Mint*, in the *Tower of London* ;

"That, whereas fome people defire to have the Monies made by the Mill for the future, that your Honours did order *David Ramage*, one of our fellows, to fet down the loweft rate that we could afford to make monies, as fair and beautiful as the prefent *Louis*, and *Car d'Ecues*, or as any coins of the *French* Nation are at this day. And,

" Whereas we have nine pence *per* pound weight *Troy*, for working the prefent monies in filver by the *Hammer*, we do undertake for ourfelves and our Company, to make fair *mill'd* money for twelve pence the pound weight *Troy*; and to make it as fair as any milled money current in Chriftendom.

" Whereas we have two fhillings five pence for making of the pound weight *Troy* of *Gold*, and the State hath fifteen fhillings for the coinage; we will for our Company undertake

⁹ See *Violet*, as before.

to

to make fair *milled Gold*, as fair as the gold coins in *France*, for five fhillings the pound weight, if it be the State's plea-fure that they will have it fo made.

" That whereas we are an ancient Corporation and Company fettled by Charter, for many hundred years paft; and in re-gard we undertake to do it as exactly as any *Frenchman* in the world, and at a cheaper price than the *Frenchman* has offered ; we being willing and defirous to put it to the trial between *David Ramage* and our fellow Moniers, and the *Frenchman*, if the State pleafe to command us.

8 *Feb.* 1650-1.   *Simon Corbet,* M. *Garret,*
                          T. Brook, &c."

" At the Committee of the *Mint,* for the tryal between *David Ramage* and *Peter Blondeau.*

" It is ordered, that they make Patterns to prefent to the Committee, with this Motto.

TRUTH. AND. PEACE. 1651.

" The Impreffion the *State's Arms* ; as upon a XX Shilling Gold Piece. Two of the fame in Silver, in value half a Crown. Two of the fame pieces are to be made with *graning* about the edge, without the Motto.

" The Moniers are to give in their Propofition the . . Day of *July* following. The *Frenchman* is to make the like, and prefent it to the Committee, on the fame day, or fooner.

James Harrington [r]."

[r] Chairman of the Committee.

I   " Mafter

"Mafter *Simon* is to fend to *David Ramage's* Office in the Tower, on *Monday* next, two Rollers, and a drawing Mill.

J. H.

"Mafter *Violet* is defired to go to Mafter *Simon*, from the Committee for the Mint, upon *Tuefday* next, for thofe tools; if he do not deliver them on *Monday* according to the above order.

May 8, 1651.

J. H."

"To Sir *J. Harrington*.

"A Letter from *David Ramage*; to fignify by warrant your pleafure to Mafter *Simon*, to deliver certain puncheons of the State's Arms, and Tools for that ufe to *D. Ramage*.

May 27, 1651.

Whiteball, June 14, 1651.

"To *David Ramage*.

Thefe are to authorize you, to make fome patterns, as broad as a Shilling, a Half Crown, a Twenty Shilling Piece of Gold, in a Mill; and if you can do it, with letters about the edge; or other ways, according to Queen *Elizabeth's* patterns of milled Money, or any other models, or pieces, you are to make; that fo the Committee of the Mint may fee what is fitteft to prefent the Committee of State, for the more handfome making of the monies for the honor of this Commonwealth.

James Harrington,
Thomas Chaloner."

Plate

Plate XIII. (E.) A Pattern Piece of the Moniers in Silver ; the Arms of the State, a Crofs in a Shield, on one fide ; on the other, a Harp in a Shield ; and both fides infcribed,

TRUTH. AND. PEACE.

And the fame Motto alfo upon the edge, and a Star for the mint mark.

(D.) Another Pattern Piece made by the Moniers in Silver, of the fize of a milled Shilling, with the Arms of the State in a Shield adorned with Laurels, on one fide.

THE. COMMON-WEALTH. OF. ENGLAND.

With a Star for the Mint Mark.

On the other Side, an Angel fupporting the Arms of *England* and *Ireland* in two Shields.

GAURDED. WITH. ANGELES. 1651 ͬ.

The computation Mr. *Violet* makes, that the expence to the State of a dozen pattern-pieces, was an hundred pounds, agrees pretty well with the following

"*Accompt of the Moniers of the Mint of the Common-wealth, upon Trial with* Peter Blondeau, *about making of Monies for Patterns.*

	l.	*s.*	*d.*
For Tools, Gold and Silver, and other Expences,	87	18	5
One Penny *per.* pound weight, for Silver,	12	16	7
Six Pence, for Gold, upon one pound weight,	6	9	0
	107	4	0

ͬ The Device of an Angel for the Supporter of the Arms feems to be taken from a Gold Coin ſtruck in *France* in the reign of our *Henry* VI. See *Figure de Monnoyes de France, par Hautin*, 4°, 1619. p. 125, 131. Alfo, *Traité Hiſtorique de Monnoyes de France, par M. le Blanc.* 4°, p. 244.

The

The Subſtance of Violet's *Petition offered to the State,* 15 *Nov.*
1651.

8 *December*, 1652, a liſt of the *Provoſt, Simon, Corbet,* and
Fellow Moniers; being in number 59; of them, 51 labourers.

No mention of the Gravers, although Mr. *Simon* and others
were then in the ſervice of the Mint.

Blondeau propoſes, that the invention of milling after his
ſecret manner needed not to be made publick, if it be not
the pleaſure of the State; and that the engines wherewith
the rims were marked might be kept ſecret amongſt few
men, who ſhould be ſworn to keep it concealed; and ſo it
is ſtill continued.

The Moniers of the Mint, ſays *Blondeau* in his *Memorand.*
did obtain an order for me to make trial in the Mint; the
Moniers hoping thereby they ſhould be able to diſcover the
ſecret: accordingly I did work there, but they could not
come at their end, only they have made ſome few pieces after
the old manner. But to prevent their further diſcovery, he re-
moved his engines to an houſe in the Strand, *Jan.* 25, 1652-3.

In the Corporation of Moniers' anſwer, they deſire
that *Blondeau* may be proſecuted for making and counter-
feiting monies of the ſame form, ſtamp, weight, and
value as the monies coined in the Mint for the Common-
wealth, without an Act of Parliament, or a Commiſſion under
the Great Seal of the State, or Common-wealth, contrary to
the laws of the land and ſtatutes in being; he having alſo
coined monies; Half Crowns, Shillings, and Six-pences, which
he cauſed to be made in a private houſe in the Strand.

Therefore the Moniers threatened him in ſeveral ways;
upbraiding him with a former caſe of the like kind: *Peter
Blondeau, what became of the coiner that made milled monies*

E   *in*

in Queen Elizabeth's *time?* The Queen and her Council, liked very well the way of making milled money, within her Mint in the Tower of *London:* But, when fhe knew, and had it proved, that the *Monfieur* who coined her milled money in the Mint did alfo at the fame time counterfeit and make milled money out of the Mint, all his friends at court could not fave him, though he had many, (as *Blondeau* might have) but according to the ftrict laws of this nation, he was condemned to death, and did fuffer execution[t].

This Affair has been drawn out to a greater Length than was intended; but being fo circumftantial in this cafe, I hope the Reader will excufe it.

[t] His Name was *Philip Meftrel,* a Frenchman, who fuffered death, 17 *Jan.* 1569. See Stow's Annals, p. 662.

Oliver's *Milled Monies.*

PLATE XIV. Some of his Monies in Gold and Silver were dated 1656; when it appeared that *Simon* became perfect mafter of *Blondeau's* fecrets in milling: and afterwards in 1658, as the Crown Piece (A) is dated, with this motto on the edge,

HAS. NISI. PERITVRVS. MIHI. ADIMAT. NEMO.

The Half Crown (B) the Shilling (C) and the Six-pence (D) are grained on the edges; with his Head and Titles on one fide, and the Arms quarterly on the reverfe. They are all rare to be feen, fairly preferved, but the laft is exceeding fcarce.

I

OLIVER LORD PROTECTOR'S MILL'D MONEYS 1658.

MEDALS

Medals of the Lord LOUDON, *&c.*

Plate XV.

AS the design of this Collection and Descriptions is rather to explain each sculpture represented, than to form a regular succession of time and affairs; I propose to give some account here of some *Medals* of certain eminent persons relating to the Government; beginning with those I have met with, and delineated from some preserved in the cabinets of the curious.

And as these times of action for and against the Republic or change of monarchical Government frequently employed and encouraged many men of learning, parts, and capacity, as the Public was affected more or less, so the use of Medals was multiplied, and they were then more handed about to denote their respective leaders, in favour of the parties they espoused. Upon such occasions many were executed by *Thomas Simon* the Engraver of Medals, and some other from models in wax, after the life, by *Abraham Simon*, and cast in Gold and Silver; this last artist being in high repute at the same time with his brother, who often highly repaired his works.

In this Plate (A) is a medal of Lord *Loudon*, from a model of *Abraham Simon*, cast and repaired in Silver; a cap on his head, and A. S. under the shoulder. On the other side, IOHAN. COM. LOUDON. SUMMUS. SCOTIÆ. CANCELLARIUS. 1645. The Medal is of the same size as the engraving.

The next, (B) an oval Silver Medal, has a bust in armour, inscribed,

NON. VIR. SED. VIRTVS.

E 2 The

The Reverfe in an efcutcheon a chevron between three
griffins heads ernfed charged with three caftles, circumfcribed,

FOR. KING. AND. PARLIAMENT. 1644 ".

The next, (C a Silver round Medal of the Lord *Inchinquin*.
The Reverfe infcribed,

1646. HON: D: MOR: BAR. DINCHINQUIN D. PRÆSES. PROV.
MOMONIE. Æ^T. 30.

Between thefe is a fmaller oval Medal, (D) with a
laurel border about it containing the buft in armour of
Edward Montagu, Lord *Kimbolton*; On the Reverfe, the
Earl's arms in a fhield, three lozenges in fefs; and over it
an Earl's coronet.

The laft in this Plate, (E) is a curious round Medal
of Sir *James Harrington*; containing on one fide, his
head, with a fcarf about his fhoulder, and on the Reverfe,
this Infcription,

THE. EFFIGIES. OF. S^R. IAMES. HARRINGTON.
OF. SWEAKLEY. IN. Y COV. OF. MID. K^N. &
BAR. MAI. GEN. OF. Y. FORCES. OF. Y:
CITTIES. OF. LONDON. & WESTMINSTER. AT. Y.
BATTELL. OF. NEWBERY. IN. 1644. A MEMBER.
OF. PARLIAMENT. FOR. Y. COV. OF. RUTLAND. &
ONE. OF. Y. COUNCEL. OF. STATE.
AGED. 45.
1653.

" In the printed Catalogue of the late Earl of *Oxford's* Coins and Medals, Page 36, this
Medal is faid to have been ftruck for Alderman *Brown*.

GOLD MEDALS *given to Sea Commanders.*

Medals of Ships, Sea Fights, &c.

Given to Naval Commanders.

Plate XVI.

ANOTHER laudable encouragement given to perfons of merit in the fervice of the Common-wealth,
efpecially Sea Officers, was by publick honour in Chains
of Gold with Medals appendant thereto to be conftantly
worn. Many of thefe were given by order of the Council
of State, and by the hands of *Oliver*, Lord Protector.

I. An oval Medal in Gold*, reprefenting on one fide,
feveral fhips, with this Infcription in two lines at top;

SERVICE. DONE. AGAINST. SIX. SHIPS;
IULY. Y. 31. & AUGUST. Y. 1. 1650.

On the Reverfe, an anchor with its cordage, and three
efcutcheons with the arms of *England*, *Scotland*, and
Ireland appendant on the beam; infcribed at top

MERUISTI.

II. The next is a large weighty Gold Medal given to
Admiral *Blake*, after a terrible fight and victory at fea, on the
31ft of *July* 1653, in which General *Monck* was Commander;
Blake Admiral; *Pen* Vice Admiral; and *Lawfon* Rear Admiral. Captain *Peacock* of the *Triumph* was wounded in this
fight, *Van Trump* was killed, and at leaft four thoufand
five hundred *Dutch* flain and wounded: and it is certain
that, of one hundred and twenty fail, there returned but
ninety into the *Texel*. This Medal reprefents a fleet of

---

* Mr. *Ames* fhewed fuch an one in Silver to the Society of Antiquaries, 1759.

fhips

fhips curioufly difplayed in this fmall compafs; and on the other fide, the arms of *England*, *Scotland*, and *Ireland*, in three fhileds, exactly as in the former. The magnitude of this Medal is increafed by an additional border, whereon are engraved naval and military trophies [x] [*]. This is drawn from a fair and moft valuable Medal in the Poffeffion of Dr. *Meade* [+].

III. Another oval Gold Medal, without the prominent border; exhibiting the fleet of fhips as before; and in the vacant fpace over them, infcribed or rather engraved after it was ftruck,

FOR EMINENT SERVICE IN SAVING

Y TRIUMPH. FIRED. IN. FIGHT.

W Y DUTCH IN JULY 1653 [‡].

The Reverfes of thefe Medals are alike, and on the beam of the anchor there is infcribed T. S. the initial letters of the artift's name. " *Auguft* the 8th, 1653. The Houfe ordered feveral Gold Chains to be fent to General *Blake*, and General *Monck*, as a mark of favour from the Parliament, and in token of their good acceptance of the eminent fervices performed by them againft the *Dutch*; and likewife to the Viceadmiral *Pen*, and Rear-admiral *Lawfon*, upon the fame confideration; and fome other Chains, to be given to the four flag-officers; and Medals to be beftowed among the officers of the fleet, as a mark of the Parliament's favour, and good acceptance of their fervice [y]."

[x] Befides feveral of the fame kind, I have feen one, in the late Lord *Colerain's* Cabinet of coins at his houfe in *Tottenbam* near *London*. Another of thefe Medals was in the Poffeffion of *J. Ames*, Sec. of the Soc. of *Antiquaries*, London, ——[*] who had the original commiffion, appointing his grandfon *Jofeph Ames*, captain of the *Somerfet* man of war, figned by the Commiffioners of the Admiralty, *H. Vane*, *George Thomfan*, and *Jofeph Carew*, 1653, and the inftructions of *Robert Blake*, *Richard Deane*, and *George Moncke*, *March* 31, 1653, to the faid captain among others.

[*] The lion rampant in a fhield in this border may be the arms of *Cromwell*.

[+] Sold for twenty guineas.

[‡] The Triumph was fo effectually fired that moft of her crew threw themfelves into the fea, yet thofe who ftaid behind were fo lucky as to put it out. *Campb.* Lives of Admirals, p. 184.

[y] See *Henry Scobell's* Acts of Parliament, 1653. 4to.

The

The GREAT SEAL of the LORD PROTECTOR.
made by T. Simon.

PROTECTOR · OLIVARIVS · D̄N̄I · GRA · REIP · ANGLIÆ · SCOTIÆ · ET · HIBERNIÆ &c

A distant View of the
City of LONDON with the
River of THAMES & the BRIDGE
over it.

Vertue f.

Reverse of the LORD PROTECTOR'S Great Seal, made by T. Simon.

These ARMES are, Quarterly, the CROSS of ENGLAND, the Saltier Cross, for SCOTLAND, and the HART, for IRELAND. The Inescochion being the Family Armes of CROMWELL.

Virtue f.

XIX

The GREAT SEAL

For SCOTLAND

ANGLIÆ · 1656 · MAGNVM · SIGILLVM · SCOTIÆ

OLIVARIVS · DEI · GRA · REIP · ANGLIÆ · SCOTIÆ · ET · HIBERNIÆ · &c · PROTECTOR

being made during the Government of the Lord PROTECTOR

OLIVER CROMWELL 1656

Gertua

The GREAT SEAL of the Lord PROTECTOR.

Plate XVII. XVIII. XIX.

WHEN *Oliver Cromwell* became Lord Protector, the 22d of *April* 1653; for his ufe, and the public acts under his government, having difcharged the Parliament, or Common-wealth, he had this broad Seal made by *Thomas Simon*; reprefenting himfelf in armour, on horfeback, his truncheon in his right hand. Underneath appears. the river *Thames*, the city of *London*, and the bridge. Behind him, in a fhield, are the arms of the Common-wealth. The Seal is circumfcribed, .

OLIVARIUS. DEI. GRA. REIP. ANGLIÆ. SCOTIÆ. ET. HIBERNIÆ. ETC. PROTECTOR.

Plate XVIII. The Reverfe of the Lord Protector's Great Seal; being the arms of *England*, *Scotland*, and *Ireland*, quarterly; with his paternal coat in the middle: fupported by a Lion and a Dragon. For the Creft, on a Helmet in front a Royal Crown or Diadem, a Lion paffant, regardant, crowned; with this motto at bottom,

PAX QUÆRITUR BELLO.

And the Circumfcription,

MAGNUM. SIGILLUM. REIPUB. ANGLIÆ. SCOTIÆ. ET. HIBERNJÆ. &c ².

² This Seal, like the other Great Seals, is fix Inches in diameter. A fair Impreffion of it was in the *Harleian* Collection. * (Dr. *Rawlinfon* fhewed the Society of Antiquaries, 1742, a caft of this great feal in brafs, and obferved that the fame feal ferved for *Richard Cromwell*, by the alteration of OLIVARIUS into RICARDUS. But fee hereafter)—— There was alfo a Privy Seal for *Oliver Cromwell*, which is engraved Plate XXXVIII.

Plate

Plate XIX. As the Protector and the Parliament had endeavoured to unite the kingdom of *England* and *Scotland* together; fo, to exprefs that union, it was by his manage-ment and concurrence ordered, that this Seal, with others, for *Scotland,* fhould be made by *Simon* for their ufe: On one fide is reprefented himfelf on horfeback, with a view of *Edinburgh* Caftle, and armies marching; with a profpect of the fhips in the river *Leith.* And in a fhield behind him, the Crofs of *Scotland,* furmounted with his paternal arms. The Seal is circumfcribed,

OLIVARIVS. DEI. GRA. REIP. ANGLIÆ. SCOTIÆ. ET. HIBERNIÆ. &c. PROTECTOR.

The Reverfe, on the fame Plate, is the arms of *Scotland,* fupported by the Lion and the Dragon, circumfcribed, ·

MAGNUM. SIGILLUM. SCOTIÆ. 1656 ².

* This Seal, fomewhat lefs than the former, is only five inches over.
* Dr. *Mortimer* fhewed and gave the Society of Antiquaries a plaifter caft of it, 1736.

MEDALS

MEDALS,

Plate XX.

From the Cabinet of

MAURICE JOHNSON Efq;

Secretary of the Gentlemen's Society at *Spalding*.

A MEDAL of General *Lambert.* A profile head in the Roman tafte ; " *which, when engraved, will do your work and* Simon's *good credit*[x]." This Medal in Silver, is in the poffeffion of the heir of the family, from whence this caft was made.

The other Silver Medal, in oval, environed with Rofes, is of General *Roffiter* ; his Buft in armour, with a collar band : " *This General was my County-man*; *to whom my* " *Grandfather, when but juft a man, was Commiffary. He* " *was afterwards Sir* Edward Roffiter, *Knight*[y]."

Amongft the many Works of *Simon*, that have paffed under my confideration, I found myfelf obliged to infert thefe three Medals in this Plate, as they came lately to hand. They belong more properly to the end of this work; but are placed here, nearer the time in which the perfons whom they reprefent figured.

[x] From a Letter of *Maurice Johnfon* of *Spalding* Efq; S.G.S. dated *April,* 1653.
[y] *Idem.* He was of *Somerby*, in the County of *Lincoln*, and married *Jane* Daughter of Sir *Richard Samwell* of *Upton*, in the County of *Northampton*, Bart. (Baronet. IV. 585.) He commanded the Lincolnfhire troops, and with Pointz befieged Shafford-houfe 1645 (Clarend. II. 719, 722); and afterwards concurred with Fairfax and Monk in the Reftoration. (Baker's Chron. Ed. 1670. Reign of Charles II.)

F

On

On the fame Plate, are reprefented feveral Cyphers, or Signatures, briefly to diftinguifh or fignify the perfons to whom I have been chiefly obliged for their communications to this Work.

Án oval Medal, caft from a Model; being the face of *James Afh*, Efq. Member of Parliament for *Bath* in 1640; and afterwards in 1656: alfo Recorder of the faid City; and one of the Committee at *Guildhall* for Compounders Eftates; circumfcribed,

JACOBUS. ASHEUS. ÆT. 56.

*** A medal, whofe reverfe has this infcription,

CAR.

SETONVS :

FERNELINO :

DVNI. CON :

1646.

for *Charles Seaton*, fecond Earl of *Dunfermline*, who, in the beginning of the troubles, engaged with the Covenanters, and was one of the Committee of Parliament 1640; one of the Scotch Commiffioners appointed to treat with the King for peace, and appointed Privy Counfellor for life by the Parliament 1641. He was alfo one of the Committee of Eftates from 1644 to 1646; but returned to his allegiance, in which he died 1674, having been appointed by Charles II Lord Privy Seal, 1671.

Gold

XXI

GOLD and SILVER MEDALS by SIMON.

Vertue

Gold and Silver Medals.

Plate XXI. A Medal of the Speaker, *William Lenthall*, Efq. in Silver ᶻ.

Secretary *John Thurloe* in Gold ᵃ, under the fhoulder T. S.

An Oval Medal of Mr. *Henry Cleypole*＊.

Another, in a Circle, of Mrs. *Mary Cleypole* ＊＊, the favourite Daughter of *Oliver Cromwell*, both in Silver.

A Medal of General *Pointz* †, in Silver ††, with his Head in profile, from a model in wax, by *Ab. Simon:* On the Reverfe, 1646. SIDENI PONTZ. 10000 EQUIT ET PED ASSOCIAT SEPTENT DUX. SUM. EBOR.GUBERN.

A Medal of *Henry Scobell*, Clerk in Parliament. From a model after the life, with his head on one fide ᵇ.

ᶻ In the Collection of the late Earl of *Oxford*.

ᵃ From the Cabinet of Dr. *Mead*.

＊ This gentleman's name was *John*, and he was brother to *Henry*, grandfon of *Adam Cleypole* of *Narborough*, in the county of *Northampton*. He married *Elizabeth Cromwell*, the favorite daughter of *Oliver*, who firſt made him maſter of the horfe; and on *July* 16, 1657, created him a Baronet, and appointed him one of the lords of his bed-chamber. The family had a fine old houfe at *Narborough*, which now belongs to Earl *Fitzwilliam*.

＊＊ This lady's name was *Elizabeth* (not *Mary*). She did not die till towards the middle of the year 1658. Should not fhe be called Lady *Cleypole*, and her hufband Sir *John Cleypole?* Mr. *Theobald* fhewed the Society of Antiquaries, 1728, a medal of Mrs. *Cleypole* in gold, modelled by *Abraham*, and finifhed by *Thomas Simon* whofe initials were over it.

† *Sydenham Pointz* was a very fuccefsful General againſt King *Charles* the Firſt. By this Medal he feems to have been appointed Governor of *York*, on its furrender to the Parliament's army 1644, though Mr. *Drake* does not name the new-made Governor (p. 171). On the 26th of *Auguſt*, 1645, he fought the King's forces at *Rowton Moor* near *Chefter*, and obtained a complete Victory over them, killing about eight hundred men, and taking many prifoners. In *November* he ſtormed *Shelford Houfe*, a feat of the Earl of *Chefterfield*, for which he received the thanks of the Houfe of Lords; and in *May* 1646, was appointed Commander of the Parliament Troops at the Siege of *Newark*. He was probably of the fame Family as Sir *Robert Pointz*, who in the Year 1626, was committed to prifon with many other Gentlemen for refufing a Loan to the King.

†† Mr. *Le Neve* fhewed the Society of Antiquaries, 1727, a Medal in poffeffion of Mr. *William Pointz*, Receiver of the Excife.

ᵇ This Medal, in Gold, was in the poffeffion of Mrs. *Anne Rowe*, the Widow of *Nicholas Rowe* Efquire, late Poet Laureat. *⁎* Mr. *Vertue* fhewed it to the Society of Antiquaries, 1746, as in poffeffion of one of *Scobell*'s defcendants.

Medals.

Medals.

PLATE XXII. (A.). The Head of *John Lilborne*, circum--
fcribed with feveral circular lines,

JOHN. LILBORNE. SAVED. BY. THE. POWER. OF. THE. LORD.
AND. THE. INTEGRETY. OF. HIS. JURY. WHO. ARE.
JUDGES. OF. LAW. AS. WEL. AS. FACT. OCT. 26.
1649.

Reverfe, a Rofe in the middle, circumfcribed in feverali
circular lines with the names of the Jury.

MYLES. PETTY. STE. ILES. ABR. SMITH. ION. KING.
NIC. MVRIN. THO. DAINTY. EDM. KEYSAR.
EDW. PARKINS. RAL. PACKMAN. WIL. COMINS.
SY. WEEDGN. HEN. TOWLEY. OCT. 26.
1649.

Some of thefe Medals were ftruck in Silver, and many in
copper, on occafion of his trial.

(B.) A fmaller Medal of the fame perfon, infcribed,

JOHN LILBORN.

On the Reverfe, his Arms,

OCTOBER. 26. 1649.

(C.) A Silver Medal; a buft in a circle, and the neck with--
out any drapery; thought to be the Head of *Henry Ireton.*
Round it

QUID TIBI RETRIBVAM.

Reverfe, a foldier climbing up a rock near the fea,
reaching with a torch, to fire an eagle's neft: Infcribed,

JUSTITIA. NECESSITASQ. JUBET.

He

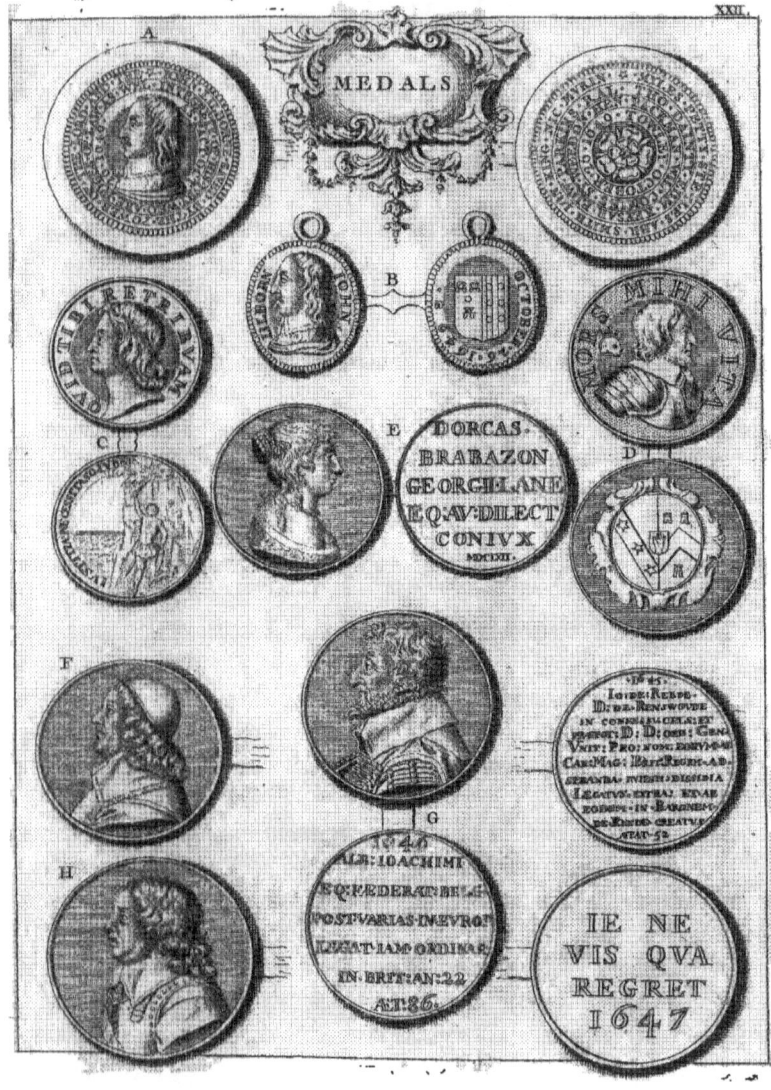

He was, in the Year 1650, appointed Deputy Governor in *Ireland* when *Oliver* left it[d].

(D.) A Silver Medal of a buft in armour facing to the right, with a crowned fkull behind : round it,

MORS MIHI VITA.

Reverfe; a fhield of his arms, three ftars on a bend: impaling a chevron between three caftles. Over all, the bloody hand of *Ulfter*, being the arms of a Baronet [*].

(E.) A Silver Medal of Sir *George Lane's* Lady; and on. the Reverfe,

DORCAS. BRABAZON GEORGII. LANE.

EQ: AV : DILECT. CONJUX.

MCLXII.

This was made by *Abraham Simon* at the expence of Sir *George.* Two of thefe Medals in filver were preferved by his lady, and after her death, came into the poffeffion of *Charles Crompton* Efq; her relation [**].

---

[d] Mr. *Humphry Wanley's* manufcript Remarks on the Earl of *Oxford's* Coins and Medals.

[*] Quære *Bampfylde.*

[**] In *Kennet's* Regifter, Sir *George Lane*, who was Secretary to the Marquis of *Ormond*, is faid to be appointed one of the Clerks of the Privy Council at the Reftoration (p. 167;) and in the fame year an Act of Parliament paffed to reftore to him the manors of *Rachline* and *Linfdurf* in Ireland (fee p. 255). Sir *George Lane* of *Tulfke*, in the county of *Rofcomon* in *Ireland*, Knight and Baronet, was fon of Sir *Richard Lane*, of *Tulfk*, Baronet, who was a younger fon of the *Lanes* of *Cowerth*, Berks. Sir *George* was Principal Secretary of State, and Privy Counfellor to *Charles* II. in *Ireland*, Anno 1672, and married *Dorcas* daughter of Sir *Anthony Brabazon*, knight, brother of *William* Earl of *Meath*. He was created Vifcount *Lanefborough* in *Ireland*, and had iffue *James* Vifcount *Lane*, who died without iffue 1724, and a daughter *Frances*, heir to her brother, who married *Henry Fox*, and was mother to *George Fox-Lane*, late Lord *Bingley*, who affumed the name of *Lane* by Act of Parliament, whofe nephew *James Fox-Lane* is poffeft of the eftates of the family.

(F.). A

(F.) A Medal in Silver, of Monſieur *De Reede*, one of the Ambaſſadors extraordinary from *Holland*, his Face in profile, On the Reverſe,

1645.

Jo: DE: REEDE.

D: DE. RENSWOVDE IN: CONSESSV. CELS: ET,

PRÆPOT. D. D. ORD: GEN:

VNIT: PRO: NOM: EORVM. AD.

CAR: MAG: BRIT: REGEM. AD.

SEDANDA. INTESTI: DISSIDIA.

LEGATVS: EXTRA. ET. AB,

EODEM. IN. BARONEM. DE. REEDE. CREATVS.

ÆTAT. 52.

(G) Another Silver Medal, repreſenting the Head of Sir *Albertus Joachim*, Knight, Ambaſſador from Holland, who had long reſided in England. This Medal has been accounted one of *Abraham Simon's* beſt performances, and has the initial letters of his Name A. S. under the ſhoulder. On the Reverſe,

1646

ALB: IOACHIMI.

EQ: FÆDERAT: BELG.

POST. VARIAS. IN. EVROP.

LEGAT. IAM. ORDINAR.

IN. BRIT: AN: 22.

ÆT: 86 *.

* It appears from *Finetti Philoxenis*, 1656, p. 155, that on "The 19th of June (1625) "an extraordinary ambaſſage from the States brought Monſieur *de Arſennes*, Monſieur *de* "*Joachimi* (both formerly here) and Monſieur *Burmannia*, from Graveſend, with Sir "*Lewes Lewkner's* conduction to Tower Wharffe, where received by the Earle of Lincolne, "they paſſed on with his Lordſhip to their lodging at General Cecil's Houſe in the Strand: "their imployment was chiefly to congratulate the King's marriage," (with Queen *Henrietta*). On the 23ᵈ of *June* they had an audience; ſoon after which, " Mon- "ſieur *de Arſennes* and Monſieur *Burmannia* taking their leave returned home, Monſieur "*Joachim* remaining here with the charge of Ambaſſador Extraordinary."

(II.)

(H.) Amongſt other Medals of Foreigners in *England*, done by *Simon*, is this, of Monſieur *La Martinay*. On the Reverſe.

IE NE
VIS QUA
REGRET
1647.

THE GREAT SEAL

OF

RICHARD CROMWELL,

Lord Protector.

PLATE XXIII.

⌐ Soon after the Death of *Oliver Cromwell*, his Son *Richard* was declared Lord Protector; and this Great Seal was made for him, in all respects like that of his Father; being of the same Form, Magnitude, and Arms; varying only, in the Face and Name; to signify that his Successor made no alterations in the Government, as was affirmed by the party who managed affairs at that time.

As it is the same, and probably made from the Matrix or Mold of the former Great Seal, on both sides, it was done more expeditiously, and with less cost*.

And the Reverse being so uniformly the same, with the same Inscription,

MAGNUM. SIGILLUM. REIPUB.

ANGL. SCO. ET. HIB.

and the arms of *England*, *Scotland*, and *Ireland*, quarterly, supported by the Lion and Dragon, as in Plate XVIII; it is not here engraved over again.

After the Removal or Resignation of *Richard Cromwell* Lord Protector, the Proceedings in Parliament with relation to the Great Seal were as follow.

* See the Note, p. 29.

Journals

The GREAT SEAL of the LORD
PROTECTOR RICHARD.

PROTECTOR · RICHARDVS · DEI · GRA · REIPVBLIC
ANGLIÆ · SCOTIÆ · ET · HIBERNIÆ · &

The Prospect of LONDON
from the South
as in the Great Seal of Oliver
the Protector.

Vertue S.

Journals of the House of Commons.

Die Sabbati, 14 *May,* 1659.

Mr. *Love,* according to former order, brought in the Great Seal laft in ufe in *England.*

Ordered,

That the faid Great Seal be forthwith broken.

Memorandum,

That the faid Great Seal was broken in feveral pieces, the Houfe fitting.

Mr. *Love* further prefented, according to former order, a new Great Seal, dated 1659. See Plate XXIV.

Ordered,

That Mr. *Simon,* who made the new Great Seal, now prefented to the Houfe, be referred to the Committee of *Safety;* who are to confider what is fit to be allowed the faid Mr. *Simon* for the faid Seal, and the making thereof; and agree with him for the fame, and to give order for payment thereof unto him accordingly.

That the confideration of the debt claimed by Mr. *Simon,* for making the former Great Seals of *England,* for which he remains yet unfatisfied, be referred to the Council of *State,* when the faid Council fhall be conftituted.

A Bill for eftablifhing a new Great Seal, was read the firft and fecond time; and, after fome amendments at the table, the Bill was read the third time, and upon the queftion paffed; *viz.*

" An Act for the Great Seal of *England.*

G

" Be

" Be it enacted, by this present Parliament, and the authority of the fame, that the Seal on the one fide whereof is engraven the maps of *England, Ireland,* and the ifles of *Jerfey,*
Guernfey, and *Man,* with the arms of *England,* and *Ireland* ;
and this infcription, *viz.* " *The Great Seal of* England, *One*
" *Thoufand Six Hundred Fifty-one* :" And on the other fide,
the fculpture of the Parliament fitting, with this infcription ;
viz. " *In the third Year of Freedom by God's Bleffing reftored* ;
" *One Thoufand Six Hundred Fifty-one,*" fhall from henceforth be the Great Seal of *England,* and none other ; and fhall
be, and is hereby, authorized and eftablifhed to be of the like
force, power, and validity, to all intents and purpofes, as any
Great Seal of *England* hath been, or ought to be."

Ordered,

That *William Lenthall,* Speaker of the Parliament, be, as he
is hereby, nominated, conftituted, and appointed, *Keeper* of the
Great Seal of the Commonwealth of England: to have, hold,
exercife, and enjoy, the faid office, to the faid *William Lent-*
hall, from this fourteenth day of *May* 1659, for the fpace of
eight days from hence next enfuing, and no longer ; and that
in as full, ample, and beneficial manner, to all intents and
purpofes as any Lord Chancellor of *England,* Lord Keeper, or
Lords Commiffioners of the Great Seal, may, might, fhould,
or ought to have held, exercifed, or enjoyed, the fame.

Purfuant to thefe Orders, there was a Great Seal made by
T. Simon, Plate XXIV. conformable to that, before made and
approved of, in the Year 1651 ; in the fame manner and
ftile with the Houfe of Commons fitting ; circumfcribed,

GOD. WITH. US. 1659 f.

In

---

f It is obfervable, that one of the members, fitting in the front, with long curled locks,
was permitted to fit without his hat. This is thought to reprefent Sir *James Harrington* ;
and

After the removal
Protector: this
Common Wealth n
to be used

Of RICHARD the
GREAT SEALE
1659

and to be exactly like that made by order of Parliament 1651

Vertue

In the fame Plate there is a fmaller Seal; the Dye of which is preferved : from whence the impreffion was taken. It reprefents in a fcutcheon, quarterly, the arms of *England*, a crofs; *Scotland*, a faltire ; and *Ireland*, a harp. The fhield fupported by two angels holding a laurel crown over it, and in their other hands, the one, a laurel, the other a palm branch ; circumfcribed,

THE. SEAL. OF. THE PARLIAMENT.

OF. THE. COMMON-WEALTH. OF.

ENGLAND 8.

and thus it appears alfo in the impreffions of this Seal, in the poffeffion of the Right Hon. *Arthur Onflow*, Efq. Speaker of the Houfe of Commons, and others. The dimenfion of it, notwithftanding the order or direction of the houfe, is not fo broad as that in 1651, from which it was appointed to be imitated : no notice being taken of the Great Seal of the *firft Year of Freedom*, 1648; probably for the reafons obferved in the defcription thereof The perfon who is ftanding, and fpeaking to the Houfe, with his left arm extended, and his hat in his right hand, is faid to be *Harifon*. The fame figure is reprefented in the Seal of 1651.

‡ The Dye of this Seal was in the poffeffion of Mr. *Richard Blake*, Goldfmith of *Reading*, who obliged me with an impreffion of it, from whence this was engraved.

* Mr. Ward fhewed the Society of Antiquaries, 1748, this fteel dye, two inches diameter, much damaged by ruft.

Scotch

Scotch and Irish Seals, &c.

ON *Tuesday, Feb.* 7. 1659. A Bill for the Great Seal of *Scotland* was read the firſt and ſecond time; and, upon the queſtion, paſſed.

A Bill for the Great Seal of *Ireland* was alſo that day read, the firſt and ſecond Time; and, upon the queſtion, paſſed.

Ordered,

That it be referred to the Council of *State* to take care and give order, that the Great Seals of *Scotland* and *Ireland* be forthwith made, and paid for.

There were alſo other Seals ordered to be made for *Scotland* and *Ireland*; of which thoſe here deſcribed were ſome.

Plate XXV. A Seal for the Exchequer of *Ireland*. The arms of *England, Ireland,* and *Scotland,* quarterly; the ground behind them *ſemée* with *Engliſh* croſſes, and *Iriſh* harps, circumſcribed,

THE. SEAL. OF. THE. EXCHEQUOR. FOR. IRELAND[h].

A Privy Seal for *Scotland :* The arms of *England, Scotland,* and *Ireland,* quarterly; the ground behind this *ſemée* with ſaltires and thiſtles; circumſcribed,

THE. PRIVIT. SEALE. FOR. SCOTLAND[i].

The Council's Seal, as affixed to an order ſent to *Guernſey* by *Oliver Cromwell*; the arms of *England, Scotland,* and *Ire-*

[h] This Seal is three inches and a quarter diameter.—* Mr. Vertue ſhewed the Society of Antiquaries, 1749, impreſſions of this and the next in lead.
[i] This Seal is near two inches and half over.

land,

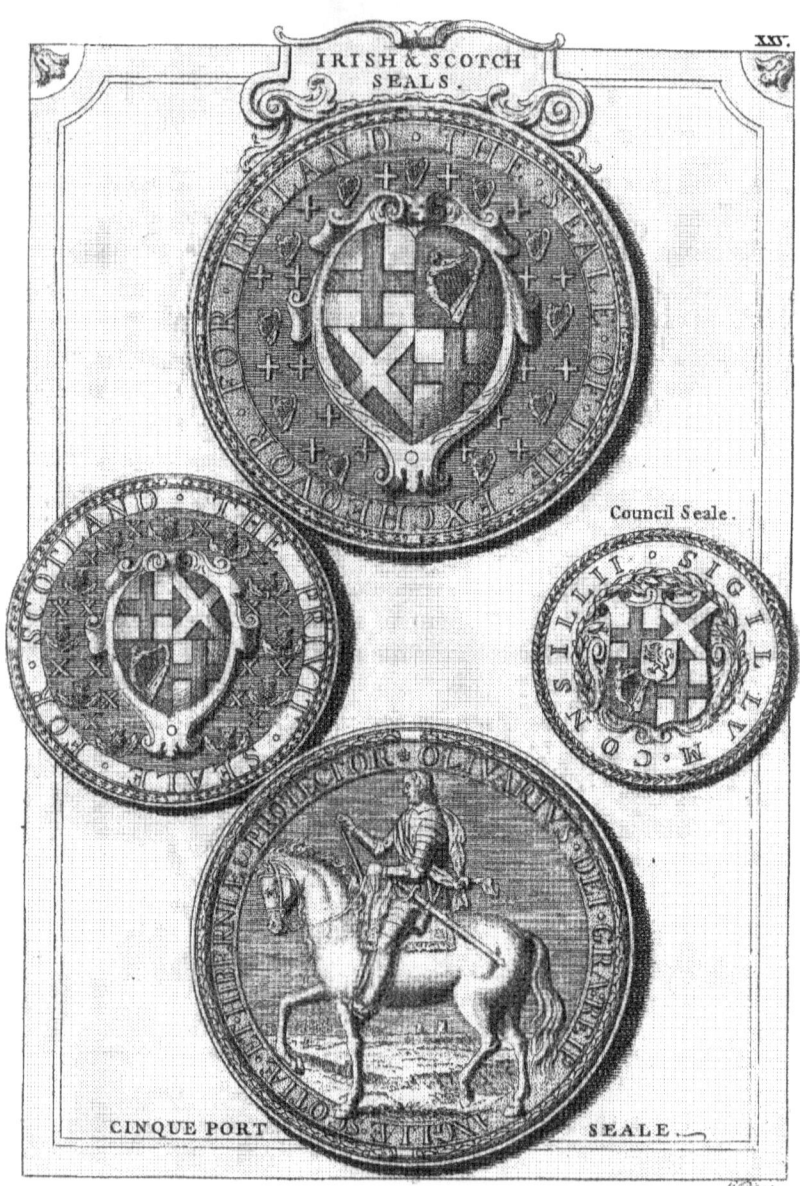

IRISH & SCOTCH SEALS.

Council Seale.

CINQUE PORT SEALE.

land, quarterly; with *Oliver's* fcutcheon in the midft. Circumfcribed,

SIGILLUM. CONSILLII.

The *Cinque* Port *Dover* Seal; reprefenting *Oliver* on
horfe-back; with a view of the caftle, *&c.* circumfcribed,

OLIVARIUS. DEI. GRA. REIP. ANGLIÆ. SCOTIÆ. ET. HIBERNIÆ.
ET. PROTECTOR *.

---

* Dr. Rawlinfon gave the Society of Antiquaries, 1746, an impreffion of a filver feal,
being the arms of the Commonwealth, and round it THE SEAL OF THE CHEQUE OF RYE.

Common-wealth Farthings.

SMALL pieces of money, of copper, brafs, and other bafe metals, having been at feveral times propofed for neceffary change, and relief of the poor, whereof fome examples had been in former reigns; and fuch effays having been, about the beginning of the fettlement of the Commonwealth, more ftrenuoufly advanced by workmen, or rather projectors of various fchemes in divers forms; of which fome being likely to be performed by *Simon*, I have therefore here thrown them into Plate XXVI. for variety, if not for value. Some of them are become very fcarce, as that called *Oliver's* Farthing, done not long before his death; therefore but few of them were publifhed, and thofe very rare to be met with.

Nº 1. The Farthing Tokens of *England*, for neceffary change, 1649.

2. The Farthing Token, for the relefe of the pore.

3. *England's* Farthing for neceffary change.

4. Another fort, with the fame circumfcription.

5. Another, generally in Copper.

6. A quarter of an ounce of fine Pewter, for neceffary change. T. K. over a fhield with a crofs. Reverfe, the Irifh harp *.

7. The infcription on this, fuitable to the impreffions of a fun and rock, is,

GOD. IS. OUR. SUN. AND. SHIELD.

OUR. FOUNDATION. IS. A. ROCK.

A. TOKEN. 1651.

---

* We fhould almoft fufpect, from the ᴛ. ᴋ. and the different crofs on this piece, that it might rather belong to a private tradefman. Snelling, View of the Copper Coinage, p. 33.

8. With

COMMON - WEALTH

FARTHINGS

FOR NECESSARY CHANGE

8. With the head of *Oliver* laureated, on one fide, infcribed,

OLIVAR. PRO. ENG. SC. IRL.

and on the other, the arms of the three kingdoms,
quarterly, with his own in the middle; and over all, the
Crown of *England*, infcribed,

CHARITIE. AND. CHANGE.

9. This laft appeared near the time of the Reftoration,
reprefenting three pillars joined with a cord, and the arms
of the three kingdoms feverally on the tops of them: circumfcribed,

*THUS. UNITED. INVINCIBLE.

On the Reverfe, a fhip under fail.

* AND. GOD. DIRECT. OUR. COURSE.

Many other fmall pieces of Brafs and Copper were ftruck
by all forts of tradefmen and dealers in cities, towns, and
boroughs throughout the nation, for many years. *

---

* The farthings above defcribed were certainly prior to the town pieces, and therefore
thofe of the latter with parallel infcriptions were probably taken from thefe. Snelling, Ib.

Reſtoration Medals.

AS ſoon as the reſtoration of kingly government came about, immediate care was taken to authorize public acts, to have the Great Seals and other Office Seals different in every reſpect from thoſe uſed and appointed in the Governments before. Therefore were thoſe famous artiſts *Abraham Simon*, and eſpecially *Thomas Simon*, then employed, to engrave the Great Seals and other Office Seals ; as alſo, the Coronation Medals, and others upon many momentous occaſions.

Plate XXVII. The firſt is a curious milled Medal, and finely wrought, by *Thomas Simon*. Several were ſtruck in gold and ſilver, repreſenting the head of king Charles II. circumſcribed,

CAROLUS. II. D. G. MAG. BR. ET. HIB. REX.

And on the reverſe, the arms of *England, Scotland, France,* and *Ireland,* quarterly; with the royal crown over them. Thus circumſcribed,

MAGNA. OPERA. DOMINI. 1660.

The next is a large Gold Medal, from a model finely emboſſed by *Abraham Simon;* to whom, it is ſaid, the King ſat for himſelf. It repreſents his Majeſty's head laureated, in his mantle of ermine, *&c.* circumſcribed,

CAROLUS. II. D. G. MAG. BRIT. FRA. ET. HIB. REX. FIDE. . . .

The reverſe, a full grown ſtately oak with three royal crowns in it; and the ſun ſhining over it; circumſcribed,

IAM. FLORESCIT.

At bottom,

23. APR. 1661 ᵏ.

ᵏ This very medal was in the poſſeſſion of the late Right Hon. the Earl of *Oxford,* and weighed four ounces.

This

MEDALS on the RESTORATION of KING CHARLES.

This Medal was defigned and made for a badge or cogni-zance, to be worn by the new intended Order of *Knights of the Royal Oak*.

The laſt, is alſo from a beautiful Medal, ſtruck both in gold and ſilver, by *Tho. Simon*; repreſenting the King's head in a wreath of laurel: inſcribed,

CAROLUS. II. REX.

On the reverſe; the arms of the four kingdoms, in ſeparate ſhields; with the King's cypher, crowned; and a ſtar in the centre, circumſcribed,

MAGNALIA. DEI.[1].

This is grained upon the edge.

Another of the ſame dye, was in the poſſeſſion of Dr. *Meade*, with this legend on the rim.

REVERSUS. SINE. CLADE. VICTOR. SIMON. FECIT.

[1] Vide Mr. *Evelyn's* Book of Medals, Fol. 126.

H

The

The GREAT SEAL *of* KING CHARLES II.

At the Reſtoration.

HERE it may be obſerved, that *Thomas Simon* having diſpleaſed the late King *Charles* I. by accepting the employment under the Commonwealth, of making other Great Seals for the Parliament, by their order, in imitation of his; it was yet thought neceſſary at the preſent, to employ him on the account of his ſuperior ſkill, and even to grant him a freſh patent, as one of his Majeſty's chief gravers of the Mint, and ſeals, with the fee of fifty pounds *per annum*; which patent was dated *June* 2, 1661 [m].

Plate XXVIII. This Great Seal for *England*, made after the Reſtoration, of the uſual diameter, repreſents the King in armour on horſeback; his drawn ſword in his right hand; with a view, as in other ſeals, of the City of *London*; the river *Thames* and the bridge over it; the circumſcription.

COROLUS. SECUNDUS. DEI. GRATIA. MAGNÆ.
BRITANNIÆ. FRANCIÆ. ET. HIBERNIÆ. REX.
FIDEI. DEFENSOR.

[m] Entry of Patents, from *June* to *Sept.* 11, 1660.

Medals

The Great Seale of
King Charles II.
1660

Gold MEDALS of MONK. HYDE. SOUTHAMPTON. See NICHOLAS.

Medals at the Reſtoration-

T H E unſettled ſtate of the Common-wealth, being divided by parties and powers of different views and intereſts, ſoon brought on the Reſtoration of the Royal Family. And among the great men principally concerned therein, the medals of ſome few are repreſented in Plate XXIX. from the collections of the curious.

That of General *Monk*, is finely done in gold, by *Ab. Simon*. His head, on one ſide, emboſſed moſt artfully. The reverſe is inſcribed,

GEORGIVS. MONKE. OMNIVM. COPIARVM. IN. ANGLIÆ. SCOTIA. ET. HIBERNIAE. DVX. SVPREMVS. ET. THALASSIARCHA. ÆT. 52. 1660.

Another medal (whereof, ſome are in ſilver, and ſome in gold) repreſenting the head of *Edward* Earl of *Clarendon*, on one ſide. And inſcribed on the reverſe,

EDOARDVS. COMES. CLARENDONIÆ. SVMMVS. ANGLIÆ. CANCELLARIVS. & MDCLXII.

Of the ſame dimenſions and workmanſhip, is the next, of *Thomas Wriotheſley* earl of *Southampton* ⁿ. His head finely done from a model in wax, caſt and repaired in gold, and ſome in ſilver. The reverſe is inſcribed,

THOMAS. COMES. SOVTHAMPTONIÆ. SVMMVS. ANGLIÆ. THESAVRARIVS. & MDCLXIIII.

ⁿ From a gold medal, in the collection of the late Sir *Hans Sloane*. He died 1667.

The

The laſt reprefents the buſt of the famous Secretary of State, Sir *Edward Nicholas*; who ſo many years, on all occaſions, faithfully ſerved the Royal Family.   The inſcription on the reverſe, unfiniſhed, is

EDOARDVS. NICHOLAS.

EQY. AVR.

His effigies, modelled in wax, by *Ab. Simon*, is well preſerved; in the poſſeſſion of a relation of the family, *Charles Compton*, Eſq.

This model is highly finiſhed, and touched, with great ſkill and art; as many others are, that I have ſeen, equal to the pencil of *Cooper*, or *Vandyck*.

The

The SEAL for the Office of the Lord Privy Seal

G. Vertue

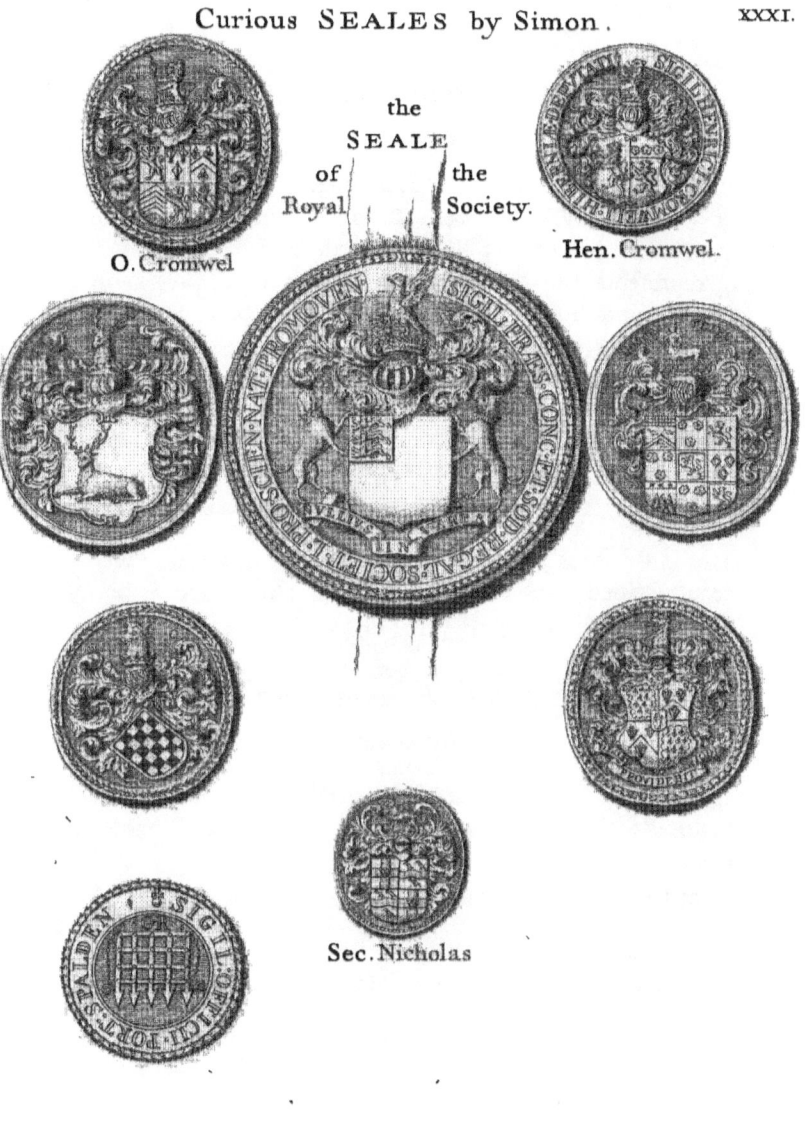

the
SEALE
of / the
Royal Society.

O. Cromwel

Hen. Cromwel.

Sec. Nicholas

The King's Privy Seal and Reverse.

PLATE XXX. This was the Privy Seal, for the King's Use, after the Restoration; and appears to be a curious piece of work, by *Tho. Simon*. It is here drawn from a fair impression in wax, well preserved, and in my possession. It represents the King, in his royal robes, sitting on his throne, and holding the scepter and globe. His title,

CAROLVS. II. D. G. MAG. BRITANNIÆ.
FRAN. ET. HIB. REX. FID. DEF.

The reverse: the arms of *England, France,* and *Ireland,* quarterly, within the garter, inscribed,

HONI. SOIT. QVI. MAL. Y. PENSE.

Over it the royal crown: the supporters, a lion and dragon: circumscribed as above, with the date 1661, and at bottom,

PRO. BREVIBVS. CORAM. NOBIS.

The Royal Society Seal, and other curious Seals,
By SIMON.

PLATE XXXI. The first is the family seal of *Oliver Cromwell*; and that opposite to it, the seal of his son *Henry*; circumscribed,

SIGILL. HENRICI. CROMWELL. HIBERNIÆ. DEPVTATI.

The seal in the middle, is that of the Royal Society; copied from the steel dye, engraved at their expence, and

in

[52]

in their cuftody. The arms, fupported by two hounds. The motto,

NVLLIVS. IN. VERBA.

Circumfcribed,

SIGIL. PRÆS. CONC. ET. SOC. REGAL.
SOCIET. L. PRO. SCIEN. NAT. PROMOVEN.

The other fix feals *, are alfo the work of *T. Simon*; and the fmall one at bottom is the Seal of Secretary *Nicholas*.

Gold and Silver hammered Monies, firft coined at the Reftoration.

PLATE XXXII. The firft and fecond, of the King's head in buft laureated, are gold pieces of twenty fhillings value; infcribed,

CAROLVS. II. D. G. MAG. BRIT. FRAN. ET. HIB. REX.

The next, is the half of one of thofe, with an X behind the head, for ten fhillings.

The other pieces are of filver, with the King's head crowned; one is the half crown, with XXX. for thirty-pence. The others are fhillings; with XII. behind the head; and in the midft of them a fix-pence. Thefe are reprefented from very fair coins, the heads only being done by *Simon*; who was then reinftated in the Mint; as appears by a patent, granted to him from the King, dated . . . . .

* The firft of them bears the arms of *John Downe*, one of the Regicides; the fecond, the quarterings of General *Lambert*; the third *St. L'arbe*; the fourth unknown; the fifth is infcribed SIGIL. OFFICII SPALDEN. over a portcullis O, R.; the fixth Secretary Nicholas's feal, his paternal arms Arg. a fefs wavy between 3 ravens Sable quartered by Arg. on a crofs Gules an imperial crown Or, which was an augmentation granted by Sir Edward Walker, Garter, 17 Dec. 1649, at the command of Charles II. which augmentation the Society of Antiquaries have affumed for their arms, without due authority.

I

Seals

First Coined at Restoration 1660.

The SEAL of KATHERINE Queen of England
Infanta of Portugal. Married to K. Charles 2. May 1662.

G. Virtue

Seals of *King* CHARLES II. *and Queen* CATHARINE.

PLATE XXXIII. A Seal, expreffing the King's fove-reignty on the *Britiſh* feas; reprefenting him crowned, in royal robes, and a trident in his hand; fitting in a car, drawn by fea horfes, circumfcribed,

ET. PENITVS. TOTO. REGNANTES. ORBE. BRITANNOS.

This was made for the ufe of the Commiffioners at the Admiralty Office.

The Royal Seal of *Catharine*, King *Charles* the Second's Queen, Infanta of *Portugal:* married to the King, *May* 2, 1662, reprefents her ftanding under a canopy, crowned, and in royal robes; with a fcepter and globe in her hands. The arms of *England* on one fide, and thofe of *Portugal* on the other. Circumfcribed,

CATHERINA. DEI. GRA. MAG. BRITANNIÆ. FRANCIÆ.
ET. HIBERNIÆ. REGINA. 1662.

Thefe were engraved from two fair impreffions in wax, well preferved, in the poffeffion of *Robert Dingley* Efq. The warrant for engraving this Seal of the Queen's with a draught of it on paper was in the poffeffion of the late Sir *Hans Sloane* *.

* Mr. Brander ſhewed a wax impreffion of the Queen's feal to the Society of Antiquaries, 1777.

The Great Seal for Ireland.

PLATE XXXIV. This Great Seal reprefents King *Charles* II. on horfeback with his fword drawn, and a grey-hound running by his fide, as was ufual in former Royal Seals. Behind the King, is the harp of *Ireland*; and underneath is a profpeſt of *Dublin*, with fhips in the river; circumfcribed,

CAROLVS. II. DEI. GRATIA. MAGNÆ. BRITANNIÆ.

FRANCIÆ. ET. HIBERNIÆ. REX. FIDEI.

DEFENSOR.

⁎ Mr. Rawlinfon fhewed the Society of Antiquaries 1746, the original warrant of Charles II. to his engraver for feals for *Scotland,* with the duke of Lauderdale's receipt. It was on fine velom, but it is not faid whether the engraver was *Simon.*

The

The Great SEAL
of
KING CHARLES II.

CAROLVS · II · DEI · GRATIA · MAGNÆ · BRITANNIÆ · FRANCIÆ · ET · HIBERNÆ · REX · FIDEI · DEFENSOR ·

At the Restoration of the King
all the proper SEALS were new made.
for the King and the Government. by J Simon.

G.Vertue fc 175.

The Crown Piece of THOMAS SIMON.

AFTER fo many proofs and fpecimens of the fuperior fkill of Mr. *Thomas Simon* in medals, coins, and feals, he being employed and encouraged by the King and publick authority, as well as numbers of the curious judges of art, it would hardly be expected by any one, that he fhould be fupplanted.

After the Reftoration of King *Charles*, his Majefty had confirmed *Simon* in his place and employment, by a frefh patent granted to him, to be his Majefty's chief Graver of the Mint, with, as was before partly obferved, the fee of fifty pounds *per annum*, and ufual houfe-room. This Patent is dated *June* 2, 1661 [p].

But fuch is the inconftancy of Fortune, and the power of variety, not long after, the *Roetiers* coming over from *Flanders* into *England*, the King, according to a former promife, granted them employments, as engravers in the Mint, with liberal falaries. But their work in the coins not appearing to be of equal merit with thofe of *Simon*, he therefore made his famous *Trial-Piece*; which Mr *Evelyn* has defcribed in thefe words,——
" For the honour of our countrymen, I cannot here omit
" that ingenious trial of fkill which a commendable emula-
" tion has produced, in a Medal performed with extraordi-
" nary accuracy, by one, who having been defervedly em-
" ployed in the Mint at the Tower was not willing to be
" fupplanted by foreign competitors [q]."

This was a curious crown piece; which I have alfo re-prefented, in plate XXXV. having his Majefty's head on one fide infcribed,

CAROLVS. SECVNDUS. DEI. GRA.

[p] From an office book in the Rolls-chapel, kindly communicated to me by Mr. *Henry Rock*, clerk of the faid office.
[q] See Mr. *Evelyn's* Difcourfe of Medals, fol. 239.

I

And

and *Simon* at bottom. The reverfe, the arms of *England*, *Scotland*, *France*, and *Ireland*, in four feparate efcutcheons, crowned, and the King's cypher intermixed: In the center, St. *George* on horfeback, furrounded with the Garter and motto, fo minutely, yet exactly expreffed, that it is much admired. Circumfcribed,

MAG. BRI. FR. ET. HIB. REX. 1663.

Here is alfo a view of the infcription and petition, in two lines round about the edge, the like never before done by any artift, in thefe words:

THOMAS SIMON, MOST. HUMBLY. PRAYS. YOUR *MAJESTY* TO. COMPARE. THIS. HIS. TRYALL. PIECE. WITH. THE. DUTCH [r]. AND.

IF. MORE. TRULY. DRAWN. AND. EMBOSSD. MORE. GRACEFULLY. ORDER'D. AND. MORE. ACCURATELY. INGRAVEN. TO. RELEIVE. HIM.

There were but few of thofe pieces ftruck. This was engraved from one that was in the collection of the late Earl of *Oxford*, and was formerly in the poffeffion of the Lord Chancellor *Clarendon*; and is now in that of *Martin Folkes*, Efq. [*] Another of the fame kind was alfo ftruck by *Simon*, with the fame beauty and excellence, differing only on the edge; intended as a Medal to pofterity, with this infcription round the edge in lieu of the petition.

REDDITE. CÆSARIS. CÆSARI.

With a Sun breaking through a cloud,

POST. NVBILA. PHOEBVS [**].

Both thefe are preferved in the higheft perfection. After this, *Simon* was appointed engraver of the feals to his Majefty for life, and performed feveral, befides other works.

[r] The milled coins of King *Charles* II. by the *Roettiers*, 1662, &c.
[*] Francis Perry engraved one in the poffeffion of the late Thomas Hothis, efq. magnified 1760.
[**] Mr. Weft fhewed one of thefe at the Antiquary Society, 1731.

In

In the fame plate is The Great Seal of the Order of the Garter. There was one made, in the time of King *Charles* I. fimilar to this [s], by *Thomas Simon*. But that being deftroyed and melted down with other plate and veffels brought from *Windfor* to the Mint at *London*, it was found neceffary, after the Reftoration, to have another made; from a fair impreffion whereof, in lead, this is engraved. There is fome little variation in the ornaments, but the infcription is the fame.

MAGNVM. SIGILLVM. NOBILLISS. ORDINIS. GARTERII.

This Seal being neatly and highly finifhed, is four inches and half over.

In this plate, I have taken the opportunity to reprefent the pictures of the ingenious brothers and coeval artifts, *Abraham* and *Thomas Simon*. Their firft fetting out in art, or from whom they had their rudiments, like many other geniufes in their early bud, has been unobferved, till time gradually expanded them, and ripened them to a degree of perfection worth the notice of the curious. The elder brother, *Abraham*, was trained to fcholarfhip, with intention to recommend himfelf to fome ecclefiaftical preferment; but by what means his ftudies were diverted does not appear. Upon fome account, or the offer of fome opportunity, he went to *Sweden*, and there by his art and ingenuity in modelling in wax the portraits of feveral noted and eminent perfons, he obtained the favour of Queen *Chriftina*, and attended in her court as a gentleman of her retinue. There he fo ingratiated himfelf, that in confideration of his fervices and merit, fhe prefented him with a golden chain and medal; which he commonly wore. That Queen

[s] *Anno Regni* 13°. *Vide Afhmole, fol.* 247.

I 2

was

was a curious collector of the works of art in painting, sculpture, &c. from *Italy*, and other parts of *Europe*; and he was one of her principal agents; for, when she went to visit the Court of *France*, *Simon* was in her train. As he was a man of small stature; of a primitive philosophic aspect, always wearing his hair and beard, according to the mode of his anceftors, the following odd adventure happened to him there.

Lewis XIII. was then king of *France*. When Queen *Chriftina* went to the royal chapel, *Simon*, being of her retinue, placed himfelf in a gallery within view of the King, in order to model his picture in wax, according to his manner of working. During this operation, the King, remarking how bufy he was, and the oddnefs of the man, did not know what he was about; but ordered one of the captains of the guard to take him into cuftody, till he could underftand who he was, and what he was doing. The next morning, the King was told that he was an artift, and attendant on the Queen of *Sweden*. Being ordered to appear before the King, he was afked feveral queftions, and being ftrictly examined, he boldly faid to the King; *Sire, What art afraid of, to fee a man, with his own hair, and a beard; which the King your father would have been afhamed to have been feen publickly without, for fear of being thought a boy, or no wife man?* Finding himfelf little employed, after the Queen left *Sweden*, he went to *Holland*, and refided there fome time. But his countenance and habit, conftantly wearing boots and fpurs, with his long fword *en cavalier*, made him every where remarkable, and to fome people ridiculous.

4   About

About this time, he became acquainted with feveral *Swedifh* gentlemen fent to *England* from that court, whofe portraits he modelled; as he did alfo thofe of fome *Hollanders*, embaffadors from the States; as that of old *De Joachim*, &c. before-mentioned, fo much approved of. At the Reftoration of King *Charles* and the Royal Family, he, with many others, returned to *England*; where he foon got recommended to the court, and to the King; to whom he was well known for his skill and merit, no lefs than for the fingularity of his figure, and his cynical humour.

On this great turn of affairs, he was employed to make medals in his way; there being then on foot the intention in honour of many fignal loyalifts to eftablifh an *Order of the Royal Oak*, as was before obferved; the King fat for his picture to be modelled on that occafion by him; which being completely finifhed in gold, the king gratified him with the reward of an *hundred Broad Pieces*. It was his chief employment to model the faces of eminent perfons; and for the likenefs or refemblance his talent was much efteemed.

Some time after, he was alfo employed to model the portrait of his Majefty's brother, the Duke of *York*, in the fame manner as he had done the King's; which when he had performed in wax, an enquiry was made, what reward he expected? he anfwered an hundred Pieces, as his Majefty had given him. But it being reported, that the Duke intended to give him only fifty, *Simon*, pretending that fomething was further to be done, for the improvement thereof, got the model into his own hands again, and fqueezing it together, entirely defaced it. This rafh and

contemptuous

contemptuous action loft him all favour at court among perfons of honour and diftinction, and little more of his works were afterwards feen. Thus difregarded and defpifed, he wafted the remainder of his days in obfcurity and want; ftill retaining the antique habit and appearance, pride and poverty, before defcribed, till fome years after the Revolution, when he died. That affectation tempted feveral eminent painters, in his life-time, to draw his picture. This medal of his own portrait is engraved from a model of his own making in wax, in the collection of Sir *Hans Sloane*. Further reports of greater uncertainty are omitted, for fear of being tedious. I wifh I could be more particular about his brother, who died fo many years before him.

Thomas Simon is conftantly reported to have been born in *Yorkfhire*; but in what part, or what town, I could never be afcertained. Nor at this day have we any better authority to depend upon relative to his firft inducements or inftructions in the art, than the tradition, that his natural genius recommended him to the notice of *Nicholas Briot*, engraver of the mint to *Charles* I. when he was ordered to go to *Edinburgh* to engrave fome dyes for medals and coins, in the year 1633. In his way thither through *Yorkfhire*, or in his return, he met with, and took *Simon* under tuition. Afterwards, when Sir *Edward Harley* was made mafter-worker of the mint, he preferred him to be one of the engravers there. The firft fpecimen of *Simon's* curious works in feal-graving which I have feen, with *T. S.* the initial letters of his name, is that Broad Seal, for the Admiralty, with his Majefty's royal fhip, when *Algernon Piercy*, earl of *Northumberland*, was made lord high admiral, in 1636, which feal, for its curiofity, was much admired.

admired. After *Briot* returned to *France*, in 1646, *Simon* fucceeded him as chief engraver of the Mint. Between the time of his graving that Admiralty Seal, and the King's death, other works and feals were alfo doubtlefs performed by him; but for imitating the Royal Seal for the ufe of the Parliament he incurred his Majefty's difpleafure. However, continuing in his office, the Parliament employed him, to engrave their firft Great Seal in 1648; reprefenting the Houfe of Commons fitting, &c. as in Plate II: befides other Seals for the publick offices; of which fee the Journals of the Houfe of Commons. Some few fmall Medals of *Effex* and *Fairfax*, and the oval Medal upon *Oliver's* victory at *Dunbar* in 1650, appearing to be done by him, it preferred him to the favour of *Cromwell*, who employed him to grave other medals, and alfo his curious milled crown, half crown, and fhillings, with fome gold pieces, in the years 1656 * and 1658, when his patron *Oliver* died. Continuing ftill in his office, he was employed to make the Great Seal for *Richard Cromwell*, and thofe for the ufe of the Commonwealth, in 1659. Being fettled in that employment at the Reftoration, he was found neceffary to make fome remarkable Medals upon that momentous occafion; and the Coronation Medal, with the Great Seals, and others, as here engraved and reprefented, till the *Roetiers* got into his employment in the Mint in 1662, which occafioned the conteft between thofe eminent artifts and him, and produced the next year that fingular mafter-piece of art, his *Trial-piece*, with the petition or appeal to his Majefty for redrefs. All that is to be further faid of him, will appear in the defcription of Plate XXXVII.

* See his appointment to this office in the Appendix.

The

The Great Seal for JAMAICA, *&c.*

PLATE XXXVI. This Seal reprefents the King, crowned, in his robes, and on a throne, with a Negro on his knee, prefenting fome pine apples to him. In the Exergue.

DVRO. DE. CORTICE. FRVCTVS. QVAM. DVLCES.

And this circumfcription,

CAROLVS. II. D. G. MAG. BRIT. FRAN.
ET. HIB. REX. DOMIN. JAMAICÆ.

The Reverfe, on a fhield five pine apples on a crofs: The fupporters, a male and female Indian. The Creft, an aligator paffant: The Motto at bottom,

INDVS. VTERQ. SERVIET. VNI.

circumfcribed,

ECCE. ALIVM. RAMOS. PORREXIT. IN ORBEM.
NEC. STERILIS. CRVX. EST.

The

The *Great SEALE for the* Lord High Admiral
JAMES DUKE *of* YORK. *Brother of* King Charles 2.

G. Vertue del. sculp.

The GREAT SEAL *for the Lord High-Admiral,*
JAMES *Duke of* YORK, *Brother to King*
CHARLES II.

PLATE XXXVIII. In the early times of *T. Simon*
he made a Seal like this for the Earl of *Northumberland,*
then Lord high Admiral, as before-mentioned, and of the
fame dimenfions with this, being at that time, efteemed a
moft curious piece of art. Yet as it was melted down,
and varied from this only in the name, titles, arms, and
other *Infignia* on the fails, flags, &*c.* but the fhip, and
moft remarkable particulars were the fame; I have not introduced it here from any impreffion.

This which is here engraved was made after the Reftoration for the ufe of *James* Duke of *York,* his Majefty's brother, as the titles round it fully exprefs :

SIGIL. ILLVST. JACOBI. DVCIS. EBOR. & ALBAN.

COM. VLTON. SVMMI. ANGLIÆ. ET. HIB. ARCHITHAL.

GVARD. QVINQ. PORT. PRÆCLA. ORD. GAR. MIL. ETC.

Over this feal is the fketch of a medal intended for the
Duke of *York.*

Befides this there is a Medal of King *Charles* II. which
was ftruck on account of the wars between *England* and
Holland; reprefenting on one fide the King's head encircled with laurel, with his name and titles circumfcribed,
and *Simon's* name at bottom: On the reverfe, the King,
riding in his fea-car, drawn by four fea-horfes, and a fleet
at fome diftance. Over all, this infcription:

ET. PONTVS. SERVIET. 1665.

K

This

This being dated in the year of the great sicknefs, it is conftantly reported that *Thomas Simon* died at that time; but where he was buried after having fearched many Regif- ters of Wills and Burials in and about *London* ineffectually, I have not been able to difcover; and it being faid he re- tired to his native country, my enquiries there proved alfo fruitlefs. I would not be underftood by any thing that has been faid in praife of thefe two excellent artifts to depre- ciate the merit of any fkilful mafters in their way, who have been here, or were eminent in *Holland, France,* or *Italy*; having only intended to exprefs the regard that is due to their performances, in honour of their own country.

OLIVER's

Pl. XXXVIII.

Lᵈ. Protector Oliver, *his Privy Seal,*
& small Head, Portrait Seals.

Coronation Medal.   *Restoration Medal. 1660.*

OLIVER's *Privy Seal,* with the CORONATION and RESTORATION *Medals,* &c.

PLATE XXXVIII. In this additional Plate, the Privy Seal of *Oliver* is like that mentioned Plate XVIII. but its diameter is only two inches and a half. The Arms, Supporters and Creft the fame as in the reverfe of that feal. But the infcription on this is,

OLIVAR. DEI. GRA. REIPVB. ANGLIÆ. SCOTIÆ.
ET. HIBERNIÆ. & PROTECTOR.

This is engraved from the impreffion of the original dye in fteel, which was, until the year 1749, in the poffeffion of *Thomas Freeman* of *Chelmsford,* in the county of *Effex,* gent. to whofe hands it came by defcent from his anceftor, keeper of this Seal, and is now in the poffeffion of his fon *Thomas Freman* of *Chelmsford* aforefaid, who favoured me with this opportunity to oblige the publick.

At the bottom is the Coronation Medal of King *Charles* II. On one fide, the King's head crowned, with his name, and titles: On the reverfe, the King fitting in the regal chair, and an angel holding a crown over his head; circumfcribed,

EVERSO. MISSVS. SVCCVRRERE. SECLO.
XXIII. APR. 1661.

The other is one of the Medals ftruck on the Reftoration, containing the King's head on one fide, infcribed with his name and titles; and on the reverfe, three royal crowns in a tree, the fun fhining above: circumfcribed,

TANDEM. REVIRESCET.

K 2   Thefe

Thefe were engraved from gold medals. The other fmall feals in this Plate are portraits of private perfons, of which kind for feals *Simon* made great variety *.

The favours and free accefs to the cabinets of feveral of my honoured friends, I juftly acknowledge with all due thanks; and would, on this occafion, more largely exprefs: But having, in thefe memorials of *Simon's* works, ftudied clearnefs and brevity; only here and there, where it was abfolutely requifite, I have endeavoured to deliver myfelf more fully, without being thought, I hope, either tedious to the prefent readers, or offenfive to pofterity, in this particular attempt to embellifh the hiftory of thofe times.

G. V.

* Mr. Nicholas fhewed the Society of Antiquaries 1723, an intaglio of his grandfather the fecretary, by Symon, finely done. Dr. Cromwell Mortimer exhibited there 1735, a fteel feal, about the fize of the head of a fteel pencil, formerly belonging to his father's firft wife, a daughter of Richard Cromwell, having the head of Oliver Cromwell by Symon.

OLIVER

OLIVER CROMWELL's Appointment of THOMAS SYMON to the Office of Chief-Engraver and Medal-Maker.

From a MS. on Vellum in the Library of THOMAS ASTLE, Efq. (p. 86.) containing the Inrollments of Inftruments of State, Grants of Offices, &c. from June 24, 1654, to the Death of Oliver Cromwell, and alfo during the Protectorate of Richard Cromwell, and the adminiftration of the Parliament.

OLIVER LORD PROTECTOR of the Commonwealth of England, Scotland, and Ireland, and the dominions thereto belonging. *To all* to whom thefe prefents fhall come, greeting. *Know ye*, that we of our efpeciall grace, certain knowledge, and meere motion, have given and granted, and by thefe prefents for us and our fucceffors, do give and grant unto our fervant, Thomas Symon, the office of fole cheife Engraver of the irons of and for the moneyes of us and our fucceffors within our Tower of London, with all and fingular profitts, commodities, emoluments, dyetts, and advantages, to the faid office belonging, or therewith had, ufed, and enjoyed, at any time heretofore, and him the faid Thomas Symon, fole cheife engraver of the irons of and for the moneyes of us and our fucceffors within our faid Tower of London, we doe make, ordaine, and conftitute, by theife prefents, to have, hould, occupy, enjoy, and excerciffe the faid office unto him the faid Thomas Symon, by himfelfe, or by his fufficient deputy or deputies, or under-engraver, to be appointed by him for and during the tearme of his natural life, with the annuity, fum, or falary, of thirty pounds of lawful money of England by the yeare, to be paid att the receipte of the Exchequer of us and

our

our fucceffors, or by the hands of the Warden of the Mint of us and our fucceffors in our faid Tower of London, to be allowed on his accompt by the
commiffioners of our treafury, treafurer, under-treafurer, and barons of our
Exchequer, for the tyme being, on the four-and-twentieth day of June, the
nyne-and-twentieth day of September, the five-and-twentieth day of March,
yearely, by even and equal portions, the firft payment thereof to be made for
one quarter of a yeare, to begin from the five-and-twentieth day of March,
which was in the yeare of our Lord One Thoufand Six Hundred Fifty-five;
and we do, by thefe prefents for us and our fucceffors, will, require, and autho-
rife the commiffioners of the treafury, treafurer, chancellor, under-treafurer,
and barons of the Exchequer, of us and our fucceffors for the tyme being,
and all other officers and minifters of the receipte of the Exchequer, of us and
our fucceffors for the tyme being, to whom it fhall or may any waies apperteyne, that out of the treafure of us and our fucceffors, from tyme to tyme
remayneinge in the faid receipte of the Exchequer, they pay, or caufe to
be paid unto the faide Thomas Symon, or his affignes, the faid annuity, fum,
or falary of thirty pounds by the yeare, quarterly, by even portions as
aforefaid, in cafe the fame be not paid by the Warden of the Mint in
our faid Tower of London for the tyme being, together with the arrears
thereof already incurred from the faid five-and-twentieth day of March, which
was in the yeare of our Lord One Thoufand Six Hundred and Fifty-five,
and which fhall hereafter happen to incurr, and for their foe doeing theife our
letters pattent, or the inrollment thereof, being produced, fhall be to them
and every of them refpectively, a fufficient warrant and difcharge in that behalfe. And if it fhall happen that the faid annuity, fum, or falary, of thirty
pounds, or any parte thereof, or of the arrears thereof, be paid by the
Warden of the Mint in our faid Tower of London, we will and require
the commiffioners of the treafury, treafurer, under-treafurer, and barons of
the Exchequer, of us and our fucceffors for the tyme being, that they make
allowance unto the faid Warden of the Mint for the time being, upon his refpective accompts, for foe much thereof as fhall be paid by him to the faid
Thomas Symon as aforefaid. And thefe prefents, or the inrollment thereof,
being produced, fhall be a fufficient warrant and difcharge unto them in that
behalfe, as alfoe unto the faid Warden for the tyme being for payment thereof
accordingly. And wee do likewife, by thiefe prefents for us and our fuccef-

fors,

A

B   C   D   E

A

SIMON FECIT.   J. BASIRE SC.

A   B   C

fors, grant unto the said Thomas Symon, for the exercise and occupation of the office aforesaid, all and singular other profitts, commodities, emoluments, dyetts, and advantages, to the said office belonging, or therewith, or by reason thereof, heretofore had, held, or enjoyed, to have, perceive, receive, and enjoy the said profitts, commodities, emoluments, dietts, and advantages to the said Thomas Symon, and his assignees, for long as he shall continue in the office aforesaid. *And further know yee,* that wee of our especial grace, certaine knowledge, and meere motion, have given and granted, and by thiese presents for us and our successors, doe give and grant unto the said Thomas Symon the sole office, priviledge, right, interest, and full power and authority of makeing, cutting, and engraveing all and singular cognizances and badges of honor, seals, escutchions, stampes and armes, wherein the armes of us and our successors, or of the commonwealth of England, Scotland, and Ireland, and the dominions thereto belonging, at any tyme or tymes hereafter shall be cutt or engraven, by virtue of any writs, warrant, or commandement of us or our successors, or by command or warrant of the lords and other of the privie councell of us and our successors, or of the justices of the courts of us and our successors, or of any other or others having authority in this behalfe, to have, hould, excercise, and enjoy the sole office, priviledge, right, interest, power, and authority, last-mentioned, unto him the said Thomas Symon, by himselfe, or by his sufficient deputy or deputies, for and during the tearme of his naturall life, together with all and singular such and the like fees, rewards, allowances and profitts as Thomas Anthony, Charles Anthony, or Derricke Anthony, deceased; John Gilbert, Edward Greene, or any of them, or any other engraver or cutter belonging to any King or Queen of England, hath, had, or received, in and for the excersise of the office last mentioned, to bee hereby granted as aforesaid. And wee doe by theise presents for us and our successors, straightly charge and command all and singular gold smiths and other makers, engravers, and cutters of cognizances or badges, seales, escuchions, stampes, and armes; and all other people, as well natives as others, within this commonwealth, or the dominions thereto belonging, of what quality or degree soever, he, or they, or any of them, be (other than the saide Thomas Symon, his underengraver, and such his sufficient deputy or deputies, to bee appointed by him as aforesaid) that from henceforth they, and every of them, doe forbear to

make

make, engrave, and cutt, any cognizances, badges, seales, escutchions, stamps, and armes, wherein our owne armes, or the armes of our successors, or of this commonwealth shall be cutt and engraven. And that they nor any of them doe in any wise hinder the said Thomas Symon, or such his sufficient deputy or deputies in the premisses, upon paine of our high displeasure and the forfeiture of all and singular such cognizances, badges, seales, escutchions, stampes, and armes, which shall be so made or engraven or cutt by them, or any of them, and alsoe the treble value thereof; the one moiety whereof to bee brought into the receipt of the Exchequer for the use of us and our successors; and the other moiety to bee to the use of the saide Thomas Symon or his deputies. And wee doe likewise, by theise presents for us and our successors, command and require the commissioner, chancellor, or keeper of the greate seale of England, the commissioners of the treasury, treasurer, under-treasurer, and barons of the Exchequer, and all and singular judges and justices of our courts of records att Westminster, and in our city of London and elsewhere within our dominions for the tyme being, and all justices of the peace, mayors, sherriffes, bayliffs, constables, wardens of citties, townes corporate, and companies, and all other officers and ministers of us and our successors, to be ayding and assisting unto him the saide Thomas Symon, and his sufficient deputy and deputies, in and about the due execution of the premisses. And further, wee doe by theise presents for us and our successors, unto the saide Thomas Symon, that it shall and may be lawfull, to and for him the saide Thomas Symon (and noe other) from time to time during his naturall life, to present unto us and our successors able and sufficient persons, to bee admitted by us and our successors into the offices of under-engraver and sinker of our saide stamps, soe often as the saide places, or other of them, shall happen to be void. And further knowe yee, that wee of our mere ample grace, certeine knowledge and mere motion, have nominated, constituted, and appointed, and by theise presents, for us and our successors, doe nominate, constitute, and appoint him, the saide Thomas Symon, to be our meddall-maker of the meddalls of and belonging to us and our successors, to have and exercise the sole making of all medals for us and our successors, dureing the naturall life of him the saide Thomas Symon, and likewise the makeing of all and singular the chaines thereunto belonging : Giving, and by theise presents for us and our successors granting, unto the saide Thomas Symon freedome and liberty to use all or any singular presses, rolls, and cutters, or any other

instruments

inftruments neceffary for that worke, as doe or may belong to us or our
fucceffors, whether the fame fhall bee remayning in our faid Tower of
London or elfewhere. And wee doe, by theife prefents for us and our
fucceffors, grant unto the faide Thomas Symon one annuity or yearely
falary of thirteene pounds, fix fhillings, and eight pence, lawfull money of
England, by the yeare, for and during the time of his naturall life, if he
fhall foe long continue our meddall-maker as aforefaid, to bee paid at the
receipt of the Exchequer of us and our fucceffors, on the fower and twentieth day of June, the nyne-and-twentieth day of September, the five-and-
twentieth day of December, and the five-and-twentieth day of March, yearely,
by even and equall portions; the firft payment thereof to be made for one
quarter of a year, to begin from the five-and-twentieth of March afore-
faide, which was in the yeare of our Lord one thoufand fix hundred fifty-
five. And theife our le ters pattents, or the inrollment thereof, fhall be a
fufficient warrant and difcharge to the commiffioner of the treafury, treafurer, chancellor, under-treafurer, and the barons of the Exchequer, of us
and our fucceffors, for the tyme being, and to all others the officers and
minifters of the receipts of the Exchequer of us and our fucceffors, to
whom it fhall or may any waies apperteyne, for payment of the faid annuity or yearely falary of thirteene pounds, fix fhillings, and eight-pence,
together with the arrears thereof, already incurred from the faide five-
and-twentieth day of March, which was in the yeare of our Lord one
thoufand fix hundred fifty-five, or which fhall hereafter happen to incurr
unto them the faid Thomas Symon as aforefaid, out of the treafury of us
and our fucceffors from tyme to tyme remayning in the faid receipte of
our Exchequer. And further wee will, and by theife prefents for us and
our fucceffors, doe grant to the faid Thomas Symon, that thefe our letters
pattents, or the inrollment thereof, fhall bee in and by all things good, valid,
fufficient, and effectual in law, againft us and our fucceffors, and foe fhall
bee adjudged, conftrued, and taken to bee for the beft benefitt and ad-
vauntage of the faid Thomas Symon in all our courts and elfewhere, although
expreffe mention of the true yearely value, or of the certainty of the pre-
miffes, or any of them, or of any other guifts or grants to the faid
Thomas Symon heretofore made in thefe prefents is not made, or any

L   ftatute,

ftatute, act, ordinance, provifion, proclamation, or reftrainte, to the contrary thereof heretofore had, made, ordained, or provided, or any other matter, caufe, or thing whatfoever, in any wife notwithftanding. *In Witnefs* whereof wee have caufed theife our letters to be made pattents. *Witnefs* our felfe at Weftminfter the nynth day of July, in the yeare of our Lord one thoufand fix hundred and fifty-fix.

By Writ of Privy Seale,

B E A L E.

Direc-

THOMAS SIMON had five children, three fons and two daughters: only one of the latter furvived him, the wife of Mr. Hibberd [a] of London, by whom fhe had one daughter married to Samuel Barker efq; of Fairford, c. Gloucefter, high fheriff of the county, 1691. who left two daughters. Of thefe the eldeft died an infant; the other, Efther, was married to James Lamb of Hackney, efq; who died 1761, and his widow is now lady of the manor of Fairford.

Some Farms in Kent (one at Gad's Hill near Rochefter) belonged to Thomas Simon, and were inherited by Mrs. Lamb, together with feveral original Warrants to this inimitable Artift, on which are drawings moft exquifitely finifhed by himfelf of the feveral Seals and Coins therein directed to be executed by him. Having been favoured with the ufe of thefe Warrants, I am enabled to enrich this fecond Edition of Mr. Vertue's work with two additional Plates.

Mr. Raymond alfo favored me with the fight of a book on vellum, figned " Thomas Simon" in the firft leaf, containing twenty-five heads in pencil and ink, beautifully drawn, and probably from the life for medals. We have only to lament that it does not appear that any of them were executed by the artift.

[a] See Rudder's Hift. of Glouceflerſhire, p. 443.   Atkins, p, 226. 2d edition.

Plate XXXIX. and XL. (A.)

exhibit the Great Seal of *England* made after the Reftoration, agreeable to the following warrant. The obverfe reprefents the King royally habited and feated on a throne, as in Plate XXX. A. and on the Privy Seal hereaftermentioned, with this only difference, that from the fides of the throne hang fix banners, with the arms of England, Scotland, Ireland, France, St. George and the union flag. On the reverfe, Plate XL. is the King laureat on horfeback, with a drawn fword in his right hand: a view of London on the back ground.

" Charles R. Our will and pleafure is that you forthwith make and prepare a Great Seale according to this draught. And for fo doing this fhall be your warrant. Given at our court at Whitehall the fecond of December, 1662.

By his Maieftyes command, Will. Morice."
To Thomas Simon, one of
our chiefe gravers *."

" Warrant for making of Seales Steele for letters of State to Forraigne Princes.

Charles R. Our will and pleafure is that you forthwith engrave the fteele fcales for our fervice, to be deliver'd to our right trufty and wel beloved councellor fir Henry Bennet, knt. one of our principall fecretaries of ftate, according to the draughts here above expreffed. For which this fhall be your warrant. Given at our court at Whitehall the 7th day of Aprill, 1664.

By his Majefty's command, Henry Bennet.
To our trufty and well beloved Thomas
Simonds, one of our chiefe gravers."

* It does not appear how there happened to be two Great Seals of England actually executed within two years of one another, as this and that in Pl. XXVIII.

The

The leaft of thefe feals is about the fize of a crown piece; the larger two or three fizes bigger; they have the arms of England in a garter, with their refpective mottos and fupporters, and round them the King's title:

CAROLUS. II. DEI. GRA. MAG. BRITAN. FRAN. ET. HIB. REX. FID. DEFEN.

Plate XL. A. B. C.

" Warrant of the 26 of September, 1664, for engraving of a fteele fignet, and two fmall fteele feales of fir Henry Bennet.

Charles R. Our will and pleafure is that you forthwith engrave three fteele feales for our fervice, to be delivered to our right trufty and well beloved councellour fir Henry Bennet, knt. one of our principall fecretaries of ftate, according to the draughts hereabove expreffed; for which this fhall be your warrant. Given at our court at Whitehall the 26th day of September, 1664.

By his Majefties command, Henry Bennet.
To our trufty and well-beloved Thomas
    Simonds, one of our chief gravers."

1661.

" Charles R. Thefe are to require and authorize you forthwith to prepaire the feveral ftamps for filver and golde, according to the draughts herein expreffed; for which this fhall be your warrant. Given at our court at Whitehall the 25th day of Auguft, in the twelveth yeare of our reigne.

To Thomas Simonds our chief graver."

This warrant, on fine vellom, is accompanied with a drawing of the fhilling, whofe face is in pl. XXXII. and its reverfe REGNO AUSPICE CHRISTO round the arms of England,

K 4

in a fhield flory; of a 20s. piece, with the buft laureat; the arms in oval crowned, and circumfcribed FLORENT CONCOR-DIA REGNA. c. R. (Antiquary Society's Coins, pl. XIV. 10.) another piece with the King on horfeback in armour, and crowned, (pl. XXXIX. B.) which was not before engraved, reverfe (C.) the arms of England in a round, circumfcribed as the firft; the half-penny with a rofe (Antiquary Society's Coins, pl. XXVIII. 22.) and void circles for the crown, fix-pence, two-pence, and penny, in filver; and the ten and five fhilling pieces in gold. Mr. Vertue feems to refer to thefe, p. 52.

" Charles R. Our will and pleafure is, that you forth-with prepare the ftampes for our Angell Golde, according to the patternes herein expreffed; for which this fhall be your warrant. Given at our court at Whitehall this 18th. day of September, in the twelveth yeare of our reigne.

(no fignature.)

To Thomas Symon our cheife graver."

In the Britifh Mufeum is a pattern piece of this in filver, given by the late Thomas Hollis, efq; which proves there was fuch a die, though none are known to have been coined in gold, (Antiquary Society's Coins, pl. XIII. 8.) where only the reverfe is exhibited. We have therefore engraved both fides, pl. XL. D. E.

ADDITIONS to p. 24.

" Thurfday, 27 November, 1656,
At the councell at Whitehall.

Ordered,
That the ftamps and fuperfcriptions, prepared by Mr. Thomas Symon for the coyns of gold and filver pieces,
according

according to his new invention; as alfo the mottos of *Olivarius D. G. R. Pub. Ang. Sco. et Hib. Pro.* on one fide and *Pax queritur Bello* on the other fide, and the two infcriptions for the edge thereof; *viz. Has nifi periturus michi adimat nemo* and *Protector literis, literæ nummis corona et falus*, being now prefented and confidered of be approved.

W. Jeffop, cl. of the counfel."

The drawing of the crown reprefents the head with the band and robe; reverfe, arms as on the coins.

The 20 s. piece has the buft naked laureate: rev. arms. The half crown, 4 s. 6 d. and 5 s. gold, not drawn. Q. if the laft impreffion was ufed.

" Thurfday, 11 December, 1656.
At the counfell at Whitehall.

Ordered,

That the ftamp and fuperfcription on one fide of the money be coyned according to Mr. Blondeau's new invention, be according to the forme now brought in inftead of that forme agreed on.

W. Jeffop, cl. of the counfell."

The drawing is only of the head, as in pl. XIV.

" C H A R L E S   R E X.

Our will and pleafure is, that upon fight hereof you fet about the making of puntions with our effigies thereupon, for the fpecies of coyns following; *viz'.* for gold the twenty marke peece, the fowre marke peece, the five marke peece, the marke peece, the halfe marke peece, and the fortie penny peece. All after the aforefaid reckoning; and for each one

of

of the faid fpecies one puntion with our effigies thereon;
as likewife our royall coate of armes for each of the faid
fpecies; and that you make all according to the draughts
herein exprefs for the ufe of our mint of Scotland; and being finifhed, that you forthwith deliver them to Charles
Maitland, generall of our faid mint, for which, and for
the premiffed this fhall be to you a fufficient warrant. Given
att our court att Whitehall, the 14th day of November,
1662, and of our reigne the fourteenth yeare. By his
majefties command.   Lauderdaill.

    For Thomas Simon, one of
        our chiefe gravers."

             " London, 20 Jn'ry, 1662.

    Refaved then from Mr. Thomas Simons within men-
tioned the punfons of his majefties furce * for the whol
filver coyne within mentioned, and likewife the punfons
for his majefties royall coat of armes for the faid filver coyne
with letters, and all other punfons nefefary for the feveral
fpeties of filver coyne within expreffed, extending in the wholl
to the number of on hundred and fixtie punfions, whereof
ther is faiven hard punfions, faiven for graving of plate, and
the reft fmall punfions for giving impreffions, according
to the within written warrand in all poynts, like as I de-
clare by thes, that I have not yet refaved anything relating to the coynag of the feverall fpeties of gold within
defcribed, and therfor the refept of what conferns the filver
in manner above-writen, according to his majefties command, is only acknowledged by '   Ch. Maitland."

    The filver and gold coins drawn on this warrant and receipt
are engraved in Anderfon, pl. CLXXII. 2; but there dated

                    * Sic Orig.

5   1674,

1674, here 1662, and over the laureate buſt the croſs of arms; on the reverſe is LIII. 4. for 53s. 4d. or four marks Scots. The earlieſt date Anderſon aſſigns to theſe from the Advocates Library, is 1664. This warrant aſcertains their origin two years earlier.

Charles Maitland, third earl of Lauderdale, ſucceeded his elder brother 1682, was treaſurer depute, general of the mint, and one of the ſenators of the college of juſtice, and died 1691. His brother John, who ſigns the warrant, was prime miniſter to Charles II. ſecretary of ſtate, preſident of the council, firſt commiſſioner of the treaſury, lord of the chamber, &c. &c. See Douglas' Peerage, 395, 396.

" Charles R. Our will and pleaſure is, that you forth-with make and prepare a ſeale for our court of Exchequer, according to this draught; and for ſo doing this ſhall be your Warrant. Given at our court at Whitehall this one and thirtieth day of October, 1662.

To Thomas Simon, one of
our chief gravers."

This ſeal exactly reſembles that for the lord privy ſeal, plate XXX. except that the ſupporters are here a ſtag and antelope. See Simon's own liſt N° 9, for which he had 40l.

———

Dr. HARRIS, in the Appendix to his " Hiſtorical and Cri-" tical account of O. Cromwell," p. 538. printed an ori-ginal letter of Cromwell's to the parliament (then in the poſſeſſion of James Lamb, Eſq; of Fairford, in Glouceſ-terſhire, now of John Raymond, eſq; of the ſame place) on their ſending Symonds to Edinburgh, for his orders
about

about the famous medal ftruck in memory of the victory
at Dunbar.   See Pl. XII. p. 13.

For ye Hono^{ble} the Comittee for the army thefe.
Gentl.

IT was not a little wonder to me to fee that you fhould
fend Mr. *Symonds* fo great a journey about a bufinefs
importinge fo little as far as it relates to me, when as if
my poore opinion may not be rejected by you, I have to
offer to that wch I thinke the moft noble end, to witt the
comemoracon of that great mercie at *Dunbar*, & the gra-
tuitie to the Army, wch might better be expreffed upon the
meddal by engraving as on the one fide the parliam^t w^{ch}
I heare was intended & will do fingulerly well, fo on the
other fide an Army wth this infcription over the head of it,
THE LORD OF HOSTS, wch was o^r word that Day ; where-
fore if I may begg it as a favo^r from you I moft earneftly
befeech you if I may do it wthout offence that it may be
foe, & if you thinke not fitt to have it as I offer, you
may alter it as you fee Caufe, only I doe thinke I may truely
fay it wil be veric thankfully acknowledged by me, if you
will fpare the having my Effigies in it.

The Gentlemans paynes & trouble hither have been verie
great, & I fhall make it my fecond fuite unto you that
you will pleafe to Conferr upon him that imploym^t in yor
fervice w^{ch} *Nicholas Briott* * had before him, indeed the man
is ingenious and worthie of incouragem^t. I may not prefume
much, but if at my requeft & for my fake he may obteyne
this favo^r, I fhall putt it upon the accompt of my obliga-
cons wch are not a few, & I hope fhal be found readie grate-
fully to acknowledge & to approve myfelf,   Gentl.

Edinburgh, 4th   Yo^r moft reall ferv^t,
of *Feb.* 1650.
                                                                    O. CROMWELL.

* In the original this name is inferted in another hand.

Since the printing of the preceding Sheets, Mr. Charles Combe, F. R. and A. S. has favoured the Editor with Corrections and the following Notes and Original Papers.

Page 7. line 2. The fun mint mark was continued only to the end of the year 1657, after which the anchor was always made ufe of as a mint mark on the gold and filver coinage.

Line 12. There were likewife half groats, pennies, and half-pence of this coinage, the two former of the fame type as the larger pieces, with the value marked, but without date or infcription; the half-penny has only a fingle fhield on each fide, in one is the crofs for England, in the other a harp in both fhields for Ireland.

The following is a lift of all the pieces of this coinage which have come to my knowledge.

		Crown	Half Crown	Shilling	Six Pence	Two Pence	Penny	Half Penny
Sun.	1649	o	o	o	o	o	o	o
	1650			o	o		'	
	1651	o	o	o	o			
	1652	o	o	o	o			
	1653	o	o	o	o			
	1654	o	o	o	o			
	1655	o	o	o	o			
	1656	o	o	o	♂			
	1657			o	o			
Anchor.	1658		o	o	o			
	1659			o	o			
	1660		o	o	o			

M

P. S.

[76]

P. 8. Mr. Vertue not accurately diftinguifhing in this place between the broad and half broad, has made fome confufion as to the dates of thefe pieces; all the broads are dated 1656, and all the half broads, of the type here engraved, are dated 1658; but there is a half broad different as to the form of the fhield, dated 1656; and another of the fame type and date in Dr. Hunter's collection, which muft be confidered only as a pattern, the &c. before *pro.* in the infcription on the obverfe being omitted, on which account I fuppofe it to have been laid afide.

PLATE X. I do not fuppofe any of the medals in this plate, except the laft, to be the work of T. Simon, but of a much inferior artift.

P. 9. l. 9. This medal is generally feen with three X's engraved over the head, in the outward circle the infcription always runs,

FOR TRUE RELIGION AND SUBJECTS FREDOM STAND, BHOULD HEAR BOTH HOUSES OF PARLIAMENT.

P. 10. Note ^k, laft line. This fhould be read, *Fortitudo ejus* rempublicam *tenuit.*

I fhall in this place take notice of a very rare medal of Sir William Waller, which is evidently the production of the fame artift as the firft-mentioned of the earl of Effex. It is in the collection of Dr. Hunter. On the obverfe is a full-faced buft in armour of Sir William: in the circle round the buft

FOR TRUE RELIGION AND SUBJECTS FREDOM STAND, BHOULD HEAR BOTH HOUSES OF PARLIAMENT.

in the inner circle,

THE VALIANT COMMANDER SIR WILLIAM WALLER.

On the reverfe both houfes of parliament, without infcription.

PLATE XI. I am inclined to think that none of the medals marked F. G. H. in this plate are the work of Simon.

P. 12. l. 7. from the bottom. Each of thefe medals is to be met with both in gold and filver.

There is in Dr. Hunter's collection a round thin plate of filver, ftruck from a dye, with the head of General Fairfax, and round it the following infcription,

THO. FAIRFAX. MILES. MILIT. PARLI. DUX. GENER.

This

This feems to be the work of T. Simon, but for what intended, or why laid afide, we cannot now determine.

P. 14. l. 6. The fmall medal without the reverfe is not uncommon, but with the reverfe is extremely rare.

P. 18. l. 18. There is another half crown of Blondeau, the obverfe and reverfe the fame as the one here engraved, but infcribed round the edge,

IN THE THIRD YEAR OF FREEDOME BY GOD'S BLESSING RESTORED, 1651.

P. 22. l. 10. A mullet for the mint mark.

L. 13. The piece here mentioned by Vertue, I take to be what is called the fhilling, the half crown having infcribed round the edge

TRUTH AND PEACE, 1651,

in the fame manner as the piece E, which is commonly called the fixpence.

As all Ramage's patterns are remarkably fcarce, I fhall fubjoin a lift, which was given me by Mr. Tutet, of all fuch pieces as are now known.

	Half Crown	Shilling	Sixpence	
Bodleian Collection, Oxford,	o			
Duke of Devonfhire,	o		o¹	¹ This piece, inftead of having Truth
Earl of Pembroke,	o			and Peace on the edge, is filled with
Doctor Hunter,	o			22 mullets.
Mr. Tutet,	o²	o³	o⁴	²³ Formerly Mr. Beachcroft's.
Mr. Hodfol,		o	o	⁴ Formerly Mr. Grainger's.
Mr. Bartlet,	o			
Thomas Brand Hollis, Efq.		o	o	⁵⁶ Formerly Mr. Folkes's.
Mr. Browne,	o⁵	o⁶	o⁷	⁷ In gold, formerly Grainger's.
Late Mr. Weft,			o⁸	⁸ Bought at his fale by Mr. Morrifon on
Mr. Lindergreen.			o	commiffion.

P. 24. l. 17. All the filver coins of Oliver are dated 1658, except the half crowns, of which there are two forts, one dated 1656, the other 1658. Snelling mentions fhillings of 1656, but I believe he was miftaken.

M 2

There

There is a crown fomewhat different from that here engraved, which has commonly been called the Dutch crown, being fuppofed to have been done in Holland in imitation of the Englifh one; and as this opinion (though falfe) is very generally received, it may be proper to fubjoin the following account of this piece.

In the Tower are not only Simon's two dies of the true crown of Oliver Cromwell, but likewife the puncheons by which they were made: the dye of the obverfe being much cracked, Mr. Arundel, mafter of the Mint, got Mr. Tanner the engraver, to make two new dyes from Simon's puncheons, in order that a few might be ftruck to give to his friends. Thefe new dyes ftill remain; and, in order to be more certain of the thing, I carried with me what is called the Dutch crown, which I found exactly fitted thefe dyes.

It may be here proper to take notice of an unaccountable error relative to Oliver's crown, in Mr. Granger's *Biographical Hiftory of England*, vol. III. p. 138, where, fpeaking of Oliver Cromwell's crown, engraved by T. Simon, he fubjoins the following note: " This piece is fcarce; it fold, *credite pofteri,* " at the late Mr. Weft's fale, for *fixtyeight* pounds. I, who know not who " was the purchafer, and therefore am abfolutely free from perfonal preju- " dice, cannot help obferving, that he appears to be far gone in the phrenfy " of Virtu. Dr. Monro, though a virtuofo himfelf, would furely in this " inftance have pronounced him infane, if he had given only a quarter of " the money." The truth is, Mr. Weft's whole fet, which was a very fine one, confifting of crown, half-crown, fhilling, and the proof fix-pence here-after mentioned, fold in one lot for *five pounds, feven fhillings, and fix-pence.*

There are two pieces, commonly fuppofed to be Dutch, the fmalleft of which is often called the nine-pence, and fometimes admitted as a fubftitute for the fix-pence, which is exceeding fcarce. As the dyes of both thefe pieces ftill remain in the Tower, I fuppofe them to have been intended for a fhilling and fix-pence, but laid afide, as was the firft half-broad, on ac-count of the &c. being left out of the infcription on the obverfe; confe-quently they muft be put among the patterns.

PLATE

PLATE XV. The medal, fuppofed to be done for alderman Brown, marked B. as likewife that of Lord Kimbolton, marked D. are certainly the work of an artift much inferior to either of the Simons. Under the fhoulder of the medal marked E. are the letters т. s.

PLATE XXII. In the medal marked C. after RETRIBUAM, is a mark for v s. (Retribuamus) and under the neck is т. s. 1650.

The medal marked D. in this plate, is of too indifferent workmanfhip to give us the leaft reafon to fuppofe it done by either of the Simons.

PLATE XXVI. To this place belongs a piece, which is in the col- lection of Dr. Hunter; it is of pewter about the fize of a modern fhilling, on one fide is a fhield bearing the crofs of England encircled in a palm, and a laurel branch; on the other fide are two fhields conjoined with the crofs of England and the harp of Ireland, and over them 1649; what it was intended for is uncertain.

N° 6. Snelling's conjecture, that this piece belonged to a private trader, feems well founded.

After N° 8. There is another farthing of Oliver, apparently the work of T. Simon, the head nearly the fame, and round it OLIVER. PRO. ENG. SCO. & IRE. on the reverfe the arms as in N° 8. and round them CONVENIENT CHANGE, 1651.

N° 9. I do not think to be the work of T. Simon, as there is another apparently the fame in every other refpect but having an R. under the pillars.

PLATE XXVII. For a very different account, both as to the artift and intention of this medal; vide App. V. art. 24. 28.

PLATE XXIX. Under the buft of the earl of Clarendo n is Tho.. Simon F. and under that of the earl of Southampton T. Simon F.

PLATE XXXII. This plate and the defcription are fo very imperfect, that we muft refer for a more accurate account of what coins were engraved by T. Simon after the Reftoration to Appendix V. §. 22, 23, and the laft article; befides which, it appears from the fame Appendix, under the article Coins for Scotland, that he did a fet of coins for that kingdom. See alfo be-- fore, p. 71*, 72*.

P. 55.

P. 55. l. 16. How Mr. Vertue got this information about a former pro-mife I cannot tell, but I believe, with Mr. Alchorne (fee his letter) that the Rotiers were taken into the Mint folely for difpatch.

P. 56. l. 4. from the bottom. There is a third fort of this famous crown piece in the collection of Tho. Lee Dummer, Efq. infcribed round the edge, *Render unto Cæfar the things that are Cæfar's*; this piece is ftruck in pewter.

I fhall here fubjoin a lift (given me by my good friend Mr. Tutet) of all thefe crown pieces which are at prefent known.

Earl of Pembroke.

Britifh Mufeum.

Dr. Hunter, formerly Dr. Sadler's.

Mr. Browne.

Mr. Cotton.

Mr. Hodfoll, formerly Dr. Mead's.

Mr. Brand Hollis, fucceffively in the poffeffion of Mr. Robert Dingly,

Mr. Ainfworth, Lord Oxford, and Mr. Folkes.

Mr. Miles, formerly Mr. Lawrance's and Mr. White's.

With the Petition.

Mr. Barret, formerly Lord Oxford's.

Mr. Bootle, formerly Mr. Selby's.

Mr. Lindergreen.

Ditto, in tin.

Dr. Tyfon, ditto.

Mr. Mafchell; bought at his fale by Snelling on commiffion.

Late Mr. Weft's; bought at his fale by Morrifon on commiffion.

With *Render to Cæfar, &c.* Mr. Dummer, in tin.

With Reddite, &c.

PLATE XXXVIII. The laft medal certainly was not the work of T. Simon. It muft be confidered rather as a prophetic than a reftoration medal, and is fuppofed to be done foon after the prince was obliged to fly this country. It was probably very pleafing to the King, as it was evidently referred to in the medal by T. Simon, engraved Pl. XXVII. N° 2.

Copy

Copy of a Letter from Mr. Alchorne, Affay Mafter of the Mint, to Mr. Combe

YOU inquire of me as a Mint officer for anecdotes of Thomas Simon, formerly engraver here; and I fhould be very happy if it was in my power to oblige you and the publick with any interefting particulars of fo famous an artift. But you know Simon flourifhed chiefly when Oliver Cromwell was in poffeffion of the Mint; and we have reafon to believe, that after the reftoration of King Charles, the royalifts zealoufly deftroyed all records of the Ufurpation in our office, as the Ufurpers had probably done before in refpect to every mark of Regal authority; for we have no official journals in his Majefty's mint of an earlier date than the year 1660: add to this, that the introduction of a new mode of bufinefs, under new officers, feems to have produced much difficulty and confufion; whence our books, for fome years fubfequent to the above period, do not afford the information that might reafonably be expected from them. The little intelligence we can furnifh is, however, copied for your ufe: To this is added, an account of all the work done by Simon for the Royal fervice after the Reftoration, from a manufcript, faid to be his own hand-writing, which has come to my poffeffion through a fucceffion of mint engravers; and thefe, with a few obvious reflections, are very much at your fervice.

Whatever difpleafure might have been conceived againft Mr. Simon, he muft have been employed in the Mint immediately after the King's return; and his firft bufinefs that of engraving Seals; for on the 10th of Auguft, 1660, a Royal warrant to the mint officers* requires that they fhould caufe *Thomas Symonds* to draw and grave all neceffary patterns, puncheons, and irons, with his Majefties effigies, &c. for coining the new money; and on the 18th of the faid month, an order iffued from the Treafury †, complaining of delay on account of *Thomas Symonde's* pretence of graving feals for Scotland and Ireland;

* Appendix I. † Appendix II.

and

and directing him to forbear other services, until he had perfected all things for setting the Mint at work. This seems to have produced a compleat set of stamps or dyes for every species of hammered money both of gold and silver *. But on the 21st September, 1661, a Royal warrant †, directed to *Thomas Symonds*, requires him again to lay aside all other other occasions, and prepare puncheons, charges, and dyes, for the gold and silver coins, according to order of the 27th June preceding: which was, no doubt, to provide for the new intended coinage by the press or screw. It does not appear, however, that Simon did more in this business than make necessary stamps or dyes for the unit or twenty shilling piece of gold, which we now call a guinea; and this cost the labour of nine or ten weeks to himself and assistants ‡. From hence we may compute the time required to grave and prepare matrices, puncheons, and dyes, for a compleat series of English coins, in the manner necessarily practised at the Mint. Indeed the task is not only long and laborious, but subject to various accidents and interruptions, scarcely to be imagined by persons unacquainted with the business!

This slow progress of Mr. Simon must needs be very inadequate to the pressing occasion of the publick; especially, when a general recoinage of the Common-wealth money was in agitation: and the zeal of our new mint officers might therefore produce some reprimand or reflection, which men of Simon's genius seldom know how to brook. Under these circumstances he might easily be led to treat his directors improperly, and they in return induced to seek for other assistance. This probably introduced the Roetiers; as we do not meet with the names of these artists till after the date last-mentioned. Whence, if they were employed in preference to Simon, it should seem only in expectation of greater dispatch. However this might be, *Thomas Symonds* was directed, by order of Council ‖, dated the 24th of January, 1661, to deliver up all tools and engines for coining then in his custody; and from that time we find no more directions to him on our books.

T. Simon was chief-graver of the Mint for seals and medals; but when he delivered up his coining tools, we must suppose that branch of emolument was taken from him. This was probably the grievance alluded to on his famous

* Appendix V. § 21.　　　　† Appendix III.　　　　‡ Appendix V. § 23.
‖ Appendix IV.

crown

crown piece; for certainly he was ftill employed to grave feals, moft likely continued in office, and actually refident in the Mint, as he would fcarcely have dared to grave the dye for the crown above-mentioned in any other place; and as it appears by the Mint Journals, that Meffieurs Rotiers were fet to work in the houfe of another officer, by agreement, which would not have been the cafe, if the graver's appartments had been vacant. T. Simon, by his own account *, was alfo employed fome months, at the beginning of the year 1665, in altering ftamps for the fmall monies. But after this we can trace no more of him; fo that, as hath been conjectured, he probably died about that period. I am,

Dear Sir,

Your moft obedient Servant,

S. ALCHORNE.

A P P E N D I X I.

CHARLES R.

WHEREAS Our affaires doe require and much import, that fome fpeedy courfe be taken to fett in hand the making and imprinting of Our moneys, and that iron ftamps and other inftruments may be prepared: Our will therefore is, and we doe hereby require and authorize you forthwith to make, or caufe to be made ready, all forts of irons, puncheons, inftruments, draughts, and patterns, and all other expediencies for the well making and imprinting of Our new moneys; and that you caufe Thomas Symonds to draw and grave, and caufe to be drawn and graven, all fuch paternes and irons with Our effigies, title, and infcriptions, according to fuch directions and commands, as you fhall receive from us. And for foe doeing, this fhall be your warrant. Given at Our court at Whitehall, the tenth day of Auguft, in the twelveth yeare of Our Raigne.

To Our trufty and well beloved Sir William
    Parkhurft and Sir Anthony St. Leger, knt.
    wardens of Our Mint, Sir Ralph Freeman,
    knt. mafter and worker of Our moneys.

(Copy.)

* Appendix.

N

APPENDIX II.

By the Lords Commiffioners of the Treafury, the 18th
of Auguft, 1660.

His MAJESTY Prefent.

THE greate publique inconveniences and damage that arifeth from the
ftanding ftill of the Mint being this day reprefented to his Majefty, and the
occafion of it being alleiged to bee, that Mr. Symonde had not yet fitted
the ftamps and tools that were of neceffary and prefent ufe; and that by
reafon hee pretended hee had other warrants for graving feveral feales for
Scotland and Ireland, his Majefty prepared and required a perremptory and
abfolute order from this board to be fent to Mr. Simonde: And in conformity
at his Majefty's pleafure, the Lords Commiffioners doe hereby order, That
Mr. Simonde forbeare all other fervices, until he hath perfected all things
which belonge to him to doe, for fetting the Mint prefently at worke; and that
he ufe all fpeed and dilligence herein, fuitable to the abfolutenefs of this order,
and hereof he is not to faile.

Per WARWICK.

To Mr. Simonde.

(Copy.)

APPENDIX III.

CHARLES R.

OUR will and pleafure is, that laying afide all other occafions, you forthwith prepare the original or mafter puncheons and charges, as alfo fome dyes
or ftamps, for Our gold and filver coins, according to Our order of the xxvii
of June laft; hereof you may not fail: And for foe doeing this fhall be your
Warrant. Given at Our court at Whitehall the xxi of September, 1661.

By his Majefties command,

EDW. NICHOLAS.

To Thomas Symonds, one of
Our cheife gravers.

(Copy.)

APPEN-

A P P E N D I X IV.

At the Court at Whitehall the 24th of January, 1661.

Prefent the KING's moſt Excellent Majeſtie, &c.

UPON propoſalls and defires of the officers of his Majeſties Mynt, concerning the fabrick of moneys, by way of preſſe or ſcrew, and the preventing of abuſes therein, on the 22d inſtant, it was this day ordered, by his Majeſtie in Councill, That no gravour, or gravers whatſoever, ſhall henceforth grave or make any originall, or maſter puncheons, matrices, ſtamps, and dyes, or any irons for coining, either by the way of the preſſe or hammer, in any place but in his Majeſties Mynt, in the Tower of London. And that Thomas Symonds graver, be required ſpeedily to bring in, and deliver to the officers of his Majeſties Mynt, all ſuch counter-puncheons, charges, letters, and dyes, and all other tools and engines for coining, by way of the preſs or hammer, as he hath in his cuſtody.

(Extract.)

A P P E N D I X V.

The Account of Thomas Simon, one of His Majeſties Chief Gravers for the Mint Seals and Medalls.

A particular of all ſuch ſeals, coynes, and meddalls, and other ſervices and disburſements, made by Thomas Simon, one of his Majeſties chief gravers, for the uſe of his Majeſties kingdoms of England, Scotland, and Ireland, and other Forreigne Plantations belonging to his Majeſtie, ſince his Majeſties happy return, beginning June the 12th, 1660.

Seals for England.

1. For the Great Seal of England, engraven on the one ſide with his Majeſties effigies, repreſented ſitting in his royal robes, crowned and enthroned with his ſcepter and globe, the

baſe

l. s. d.

bafe or bottom of the throne being two lyons gardant fupporting catooryes, on which two eagles ftand difplayed, about the middle of the throne, bearing up the canopy or top, on which two angells lye fupporting his Majefties arms, with the royall diadem or crown; the throne being adorned with frutrigefs, and the banner of St. George, the rofe and crown, and the thiftle and crown on the right hand, and on the left hand the banners of the union of England and Scotland, the flower de lis and crown, and the harp and crown: in the circumference, a fcrole with his Majefties titles, furrounded with a laurell*, and on the other fide his Majefties effigies on horfeback, in a running pofture, reprefented in an ancient Roman manner, a laurell on his head, and a fword drawn in his hand; and in a profpect the city of London: in the circumference the title in a fcrole, furrounded with a laurell † as on the other fide, weighing 109 oz. 3 dwts. at 5s. 4d.   } 200 12 0

} 29 2 1

2.   For a Privy Seal with his Majefties arms, garter, and crown, with two lyons fupporters, and his Majefties titles round on the circumference, weighing in filver 16.oz.   } 20 0 0

3.   · For a fygnet of fteel of his Majefty's royall armes, garter, and crown, and titles, for Mr. Secretary Maurice.   } 20 0 0.

4.   For Mr. Secretary Nicholas four fteele feals of his own arms, two larger and two leffer, for his Majefties ufe, for paffes and the like.   } 10 0 0

5.   For fix fteele feals of feverall phantafies, of heads and figures for private letters to forreigne parts, for Mr. Secretary Nicholas.   } 9 0 0

6.   For four fteele feals of knots, for private letters for Mr. Secretary Nicholas, for his Majefties ufe.   } 6 0 0

7.   For four fteele feals, with a rofe and crown, fupported with a lyon and a dragon, and the motto SIGILL PRIVI. CON. for the four clerks of his Majefties privy counfell.   } 40 0 0

8.   For a large double feal for the King's Bench, on the one fide his Majefties effigies, fitting in his royall robes, inthroned, as in the Great Seal, with the rofe and crown on the right fide, and the flower de lis and crown on the left, and his

* Pl. XXXIX.   † Pl. XL.

4   Majefties

	l.	s	d.

Majefties titles in the circumference, and on the other fide his Majefties royall coat of arms inclofed with a garter, and a compartment fupported with a lyon and a dragon, and the Emperiall crown over it, with this motto underneath, PRO BREVIBUS CORAM NOBIS, the filver weighing 38 oz. 9 dwt. *   **65 0 0**

9. For a large double feal for his Majefties Court of Exchequer, rough, being his Majefties effigies on the one fide, in his royall robes, inthroned, with his titles in a fcrole, and on the other fide his Majefties coat of arms in a garter crowned, fupported with an Antilope and Stagg, with this motto in a fcrole, SIGILL. SCACARIJ. DOMINI. REGIS, with his Majefties titles in the circumference in filver, weighing 31 oz.   **40 0 0**

10. For a large double feal for the Dutchy of Lancafter, ingraven on the one fide with his Majefties effigies on horfeback, and his titles round the circumference, and on the other fide the arms of the Dutchy, in a compartment fhield, fupported with grey hounds, and the ducall crown over it in filver, weighing 40 oz.   **50 0 0**

11. For a fingle feal, being three lyons in a compartment fhield, with mantles, helmet, and creft, between two feathers, with this motto in the circumference ; SIGILL. CAROLI II. DEI. GRAT. ANG. SCO. FRA. ET. HIB. REGIS. DE. DVCATU SUO. LANCAST. in filver, weight 28 oz. 16 dwt.   **25 0 0**

12. For a large double feal for the County Palatine of Chefter, on the one fide his Majefties effigies on horfeback in armes, with his titles, in the circumference, and on the other fide the arms of the Dutchy, it being three wheat-fheaves, fupported by two dragons, holding each of them a feather, with the crown ducall over, and the title in the circumference in filver, 40 oz. 19 dwt,   **50 0 0**

13. For a large double feal for the Order of the Garter, having on one fide St. George a horfeback, fighting with the dragon **, and on the other fide St. George's crofs, empal'd with his Majefties armes, with the garter adorned with trophies, and the Imperiall crown thereon, in filver, weighing 38 oz. 5 dwt.   **70 0 0**

* Pl. XXX.   ** Pl. XXXV.

For

	l.	s.	d.

14. For a steel sygnet, of the largeness of his Majesties sygnet, of the cross of St. George, and his Majesties arms impal'd within a garter and the crown. — 20 0 0

15. For a great double seal, for the Queen's Majesty, engraven on the one side with her Majesties effigies standing in a throne, with a scepter in one hand, and a globe in the other, robed and crowned with her Majesties titles round *; and on other side, her Majesties arms, being the arms of England and Portugall, impalled in a compartment shield, supported by a lyon and a dragon, and an Imperiall crown thereon, surrounded also with her Majesties titles, in silver, weighing 42 oz. 8 dwt. — 100 0 0

16. For four steele seals for Mr. Secretary Bennet, with his own coat of arms, mantle, and crest, for his Majesties service. — 10 0 0

17. For two steel plates, for Mr. Secretary Bennet, one larger than the other, with his own coat of arms, mantle, and crest, for his Majesties service. — 5 0 0

18. For three small silver seals for Mr. Secretary Bennet, two of them with his own coat of arms, mantle, and crest, and the other with a knot. — 2 0 0

19. For a large originall seal, for the Countyes of Radnor, Brecknock, and Glamorgan, ingraven with his Majesties effigies on horseback, in arms and tytle on the one side, and on the other side his Majesties arms, crown, and supporters, with the feathers and crown on either side, and titles, in silver, 24 oz. — 50 0 0

20. For a large originall double seal, for the counties of Denbigh and Montgomery, on the one side his Majesties effigies on horseback in arms, with the princes arms and titles, and on the other side, his Majesties arms with a crown, supported with a grey-hound and a stagg, with his Majesties titles, in in silver, weight 28 oz. 5 dwt. — 50 0 0

21. For a judicial seal for the counties of Denbigh, Montgomery, and Flint; ingraven with his Majesties effigies on horseback in arms, and his Majesties titles on one side, and on the other side his Majesties arms in a compartment shield, with a crown, and supported with a lyon and an antilope, with the princes arms underneath, and in the circumference this motto, SIGILLVM JUDICALE. PRO COMITATIBVS DENBIGIJ, MONTGOMERI, ET FLINT, 1661, in silver, weight 15 oz. 3 dwt. — 50 0 0

* Pl. XXXIII.

STAMPS

Stamps for Coins for England.

l.   s.   d.

22.   For fourteen feveral original ftamps by way of the hamer, *viz.* the crown, the half-crown, the fhilling, the fix-pence, the four-pence, the three-pence, the two-pence, the penny, and the half-penny, in filver; and for gold, the twenty, the ten, and the five fhilling pieces, and the angel piece *.   280   0   0

23.   For making ftamps for a twenty fhilling piece, by way of the mill, working myfelf and my fervants, nine or ten weeks time.   45   0   0

M E D D A L L S.

24.   For two gold meddalls for his Majefties two mafter cooks, on the one fide his Majefties effigies in royall robes, with a laurell on his head, and the other fide the royall oak, with the fun fhining upon it, and this motto, JAM FLORESCIT, the 22 Aprill, 1661, weight 3oz. 2dwts. 16gr †.   20   10   0

25.   For the originall emboffing of the head of the faid meddalls, and graveing the reverfe in fteel.   28   0   0

26.   For the coronation meddall, being engraven on the one fide with his Majefties effigies in his royall robes, crowned with his Majefties titles in the circumference, and on the other fide, his Majefties effigies from head to foot, fitting in his royall robes, with his fcepter in one hand and his other hand upon the globe, crowned by an angell, with this motto EVERSO MISSUS SVCCERRERE SECLO, the 23 April, 1661 ‡.   110   0   0

27.   For makihg and engraving the originall ftamp of the faid meddalls, and coyning to to the vallue of five hundred pounds worth for the prefent occafion, for the ufe of his Majeftie.   10   10   0

28.   For another gold meddall, according to the pattern of the mafter cooks afore-mentioned, for an Italian mufician, weight 1 oz. 10 dwt. 8 gr.   38   0   0

29.   For the originall ftamps of another medall, ingraven in fteel dyes, with his Majefties effigies in an Imperiall drefs, and his Majefties titles on the one fide and on the other fide, the four   16   0   0

* See before, p. 69* 70*.   † Pl. XXVII.   ‡ Pl. XXXVIII.
                                                            coats

l. s. d.

coats of England, Scotland, France, and Ireland, fingly quartered, with this motto (MAGNA OPERA DOMINI).

30. For the ftamps of another Meddall, with his Majefties
cyphers, and the badge of the four kingdoms between them. } 16 0 0

31. For a large and perfect double feal for his Majefties Court
of Exchequer, being ingraven on the one fide with his Majefties
effigies, inthroned according to the form of the new great feal
of England, differing only, that inftead of the banners, there
is on the right hand, the rofe and crown, and on the left hand
the flower de lis and crown; and on the other fide his Majefties } 65 0 0
royall coat of arms in a compartment fhield, furrounded with
a garter, fupported with an antelope and a ftagg, with this
motto, SIGILL SCACARII DOMINI REGIS, and on the circumference his Majefties tytles.

Severall things made for his Majefty's own particular Ufe.

For engraving an antick head in a cornelian *. 10 0 0

For two blew faphirs ingraven with his Majefties cypher. } 20 0 0
For the ftones.

For the graving. 14 0 0

For the gold, and making. 3 0 0

Seals for Scotland.

For the great feal for Scotland, being on one fide his
Majefties effigies on horfeback, galloping with his fword in his
hand, and the profpect of the city of Edenborough, and round
about his Majefties titles, and on the other fide his Majefties } 150 0 0
arms, fupported by two unicorns, the Imperiall crown, with
the banner of England and Scotland, with his Majefties titles,
filver, weight 76 oz. 14 dwts.

For another feal for Scotland, being the juft half of the } 75 0 0
great called the quarter feal.

* Q. if that engraved in Pl. XXXVIII.

For

l. s. d.

For a privy feal of Scotland, with his Majefties royal coat of arms att large, with the fupporters, mantle, helmet, and creft, motto, and titles, weight 16 oz. } 15 0 0

For a fteele fygnet for Scotland (being of the fame with that of England) with the arms of Scotland, firft and laft quartered, with England and Ireland, in a garter, with the Imperiall crown, and his Majefties titles round it. } 20 0 0

For his Majefties royall fignature in filver, of his name for Scotland. } 6 0 0

For two filver fignetts for Scotland, with his Majefties arms and crown, weight } 10 0 0

Coynes for Scotland.

For the originall ftamps for eight feverall forts of coynes for gold and filver moneys, *viz.* for gold, the twenty mark peece, the ten mark peece, the two mark peece, the mark peece, the half mark peece, and the forty penny peece, all in a new manner and form, to coyn by way of the mill, or prefs ingraven; on the filver, on one fide his Majefties effigies in an Imperiall manner, head and fhoulder in arms, with a fcarfe, and a laurell on his head, and the order of St. George, with his Majefties titles; and, on the other fide, four efcutchions concentring in the form of a crofs, and between every arms cyphers, being two cc's crowned, and the titles round it; and on the gold his Majefties effigies, in an Imperiall manner, with a laurell about his head, and a fcarf about his neck, and his Majefties titles round it, and on the other fide, the four arms and cyphers, with the difference from the filver, that the arms are all crowned, and the cyphers not. For making of all the original punfons of heads, arms, letters, granings, figures, and all the reft of the punfons that thereunto belong, I have only delivered the filver ftamps, and muft reckon for them as for thofe of England made by the mill, I have not made all the arms of the gold which I reckon not. } 100 0 0

O. Seals.

l.   s.   d.

Seals for Ireland.

For the great feal of Ireland, being on the one fide engraven with his Majefties effigies in arms on horfe-back, galloping with his fword drawn in his hand, and the profpect of the city of Dublin, with the armes and titles round it, and on the other fide, the effigies of his Majefty in a throne, robed and crowned with his fcepter and globe, and his Majefties titles in the circumference in filver, weight 78 oz. 14 dwt *. ⎬ 150 0 0

For three large double feals for the three courts of Ireland, viz. for the Exchequer, being on the one fide his Majefties portracture fitting in a fhipp robed and crowned, with his fcepter and globe on one fide; and the others of the King's Bench and Common Pleas, his Majefties effigies inthroned like as in one fide of the great feal of Ireland, and on the other fide of them, all his Majefties coat of arms in a garter, fupporters helmet, mantles, and creft, and in a fcrole the motto DIEU ET MON DROIT, with his Majefties titles in the circumference in filver, weight 89 oz. ⎬ 155 0 0

For a large feal for the Court of Wardes in Ireland, of his Majefties arms, garter, mantles, helmet, creft, and fupporters, with the motto and titles, being a filver feal fingle, weight 16 oz. ⎬ 35 0 0

For three fmall feals of the bignefs of a half crown filver, an ivory one, with the rofe and crown, and two of them with his Majefties armes, garter, and crown. ⎬ 9 0 0

For my journey into France for his Majefties fpeciall fervice I expended 30 l. and a month's time. ⎬ 65 0 0

Seals for his Majefties forreigne Plantations.
For the Ifland of Jamaica.

For a large double feal for the ifland of Jamaica, ingraven on the one fide with his Majefties fitting in a throne robed and crowned, with his fcepter in his left hand, and his globe lying

* See Pl. XXXIV. This account takes no notice of the greyhounds.

in

l.　s.　d.

in his lapp, and his right hand extended towards a prefent of
pine apples, prefented to him as the fruits of that country, by
an Indian kneeling before him, with this motto, DURO DE
CORTICE FRVCTVS QVAM DVLCES, the curtains drawn up, and
held by little angells, and his Majefties titles in the circumference, with the addition DOMIN. JAMAICÆ, and on the other
fide, the armes of the country, *viz.* the crofs of England,
charged with five pine apples, fupported with two Indians, one
being a woman on the right hand holding a difh with five pine
apples in it; and on the left hand a man armed with a bow,
according to the manner of the country, the mantles and
helmet, and for the creft an allegator, with this motto underneath, INDVS VTERQUE SERVIET UNI, and round about the
circumference ECCE ALIUM RAMOS PORREXIT IN ORBEM NEC
STERILIS CRUX EST, in filver, weight 31 oz. 14 dwt *.

70　0　0

For Virginia.

For a large fteel fcale for Virginia, with his Majefties arms
in a garter, and the Imperiall crown, with this motto, JUDAT
VIRGINIA QUINTUM.

20　0　0

For Barbadus.

For a large double feal for his Majefties ifland of Barbadus;
on the one fide his Majeftie reprefented as a Neptune in a
chariot in his royal robes, with a crown on his head, and a
trident in his hand, drawn by two fea-horfes, with this motto
in the circumference, ET PENITUS TOTO REGNANTES ORBE
BRITTANNOS ††, and on the other fide his Majefties Royall arms
in a garter and crown, and his Majefties titles in the circumference, with this addition, DOM. BARBADÆ ET INSUL. CARIB.
in filver, weight 37 oz. 9 dwt.

70　0　0

* Pl. XXXVI.
†† The fame device, &c. on the admiralty feal, engraved in Pl. XXXIII.

For

l.   s.   d.

For feverall Draughts and Imboftings.

For the draughts and imbofting of the great feal of Eng-}   65   0   0
land,

For embofting the King's Bench feal,   25   0   0

For embofting the great feal of Ireland on the one fide,   50   0   0

For the draughts and imbofting of the Barbadus feal,   25   0   0

For the draughts and imbofting of the Jamaica feal,   25   0   0

For feverall draughts of coynee and medalls,   15   0   0

For fundry expences and extraordinary attendances at the}
court, for directions about the draughts of feals, coynes, and }   20   0   0
medalls.

My brother Laurence **For three affiftant workmen befides myfelf, for**}
that deferved leaft had making of dozens of piles and treffells att the |
30l. of me. firft coynage at 5 s. *per* diem, working fo many }   60   0   0
days about them,

For feverall Preffes.

For a large prefs for Mr. fecretary Nicholas,   16   0   0

For a prefs of the like bignefs for the counfell,   16   0   0

This prefs is my gard- For a middle fized prefs for Mr. Secretary
ner's, who is to have the Bennet.
money when paid, and
this is promifed to be For a fmall prefs for Mr. Secretary Ben-
paid by my lord Afhley net.
to Mr. Onfly.

Here follows feverall other Seales, made and delivered to his Majeftie, and for his Majefties Service.

Auguft, 13. Delivered to Mr. Godolphin two fteel feals}
of Mr. fecretary Bennett's coat,   5   0   0

November 28. Delivered to Mr. Williamfon one fteel feal,
for hard wax of Mr. fecretary Bennett's coat, as the former; |
and alfo a filver feale of a cypher, in imitation of another, alfo }   4   0   0
the fame cypher new ingraven within a week after,

                                    July

l. s. d.

28 July, 1664. Delivered to Sir Henry Bennet two steel feals for his Majesties ufe, being one larger feal, with his Majesties arms, garter, crown, fupporters, motto, and titles, the } 30 0 0

other a fmall one, with his Majesties arms, garter, and crown, for private letters. } 10 0 0

Sept. 26. Delivered to Mr. fecretary Maurice fix fmall steel feales for private letters, for his Majesties ufe, three of figures, and three of heads. } 6 0 0

This large feal in the articles above the larger he mentions, my mafter Green had 42 l. allowed him. December 5, 1664. Then delivered to the King's Majeftie a very large steel feal for letter of ftate to forraigne princes, of the fize of thofe

I made for his Majesties father of bleffed memory when a fervant, with his Majesties whole atcheivments, his Majesties arms in a garter in a compartment, the fupporters helmet, creft, titles, and motto; as alfo a fmall steel feal, with } 40 0 0

his Majesties arms, garter, and crown, both for Mr. fecretary Bennet, } 10 0 0

Alfo delivered two steel feales of Mr. fecretary Bennet's coat, one larger and one leffer, of the fecond alteration of his coat, } 5 0 0

March 21, 1664. Delivered to Mr. Lee three steel feales of Mr. fecretary Bennet's coat, with mantle and creft of the fecond alteration of his coat, } 6 0 0

April 1665. Delivered two steel feals of Mr. fecretary's arms, being the third alteration when created a baron*, one feal larger than another, } 5 0 0

Alfo made for Mr. fecretary Maurice three steel feals, the like is made for Mr. fecretary Bennet, as appears by his } 30 0 0

Majesties Warrant for letters of ftate to forreigne princes, and } 10 0 0

one very fmall one of his Majesties arms in a garter, and the crown over, parallel to the other, } 40 0 0

Alfo made for Mr. fecretary Bennet three feals in steel, one larger and two leffer, of the third alteration of Mr. fecretary's coat, } 7 0 0

For altering of the ftamps for the four-pence, three-pence, two-pence, and penny, by way of the mill, wherein I and my fervants wrought two months. } 35 0 0

* By the ftyle of lord Arlington, 17 C. II. and vifcount Thetford earl of Arlington, 24 ejufd. He died a catholic July 28, 1685.

Directions for Binding the Sculptures.

There are *Head-pieces* to pp. 1. and 3. of the Introduction ; and a *Tail-piece* to p. 10.

⁎ Besides the additions to this Work mentioned in the Appendix, there is, in the collection of his Grace the Duke of Devonshire, a medal by Abraham Simon, of the Duke of Lauderdale. On one side, his head in profile ; on the reverse, the family crest.

P. 70*. l. 24. *for* pl. XL. *read* pl. XXXIX.